RAIN

In the Promised Land

Book 8

Rain Series

RAIN

In the Promised Land

Vanessa
Miller

Book 8
Rain Series

Vanessa Miller
www.vanessamiller.com

Printed in the United States of America
© 2015 by Vanessa Miller

Praise Unlimited Enterprises
Charlotte, NC

Other Books by Vanessa Miller

Rain in the Promised Land
Heaven Sent
After the Rain
How Sweet The Sound
Heirs of Rebellion
Feels Like Heaven
Heaven on Earth
The Best of All
Better for Us
Her Good Thing
Long Time Coming
A Promise of Forever Love
A Love for Tomorrow
Yesterday's Promise
Forgotten
Forgiven
Forsaken
Rain for Christmas (Novella)
Through the Storm
Rain Storm
Latter Rain
Abundant Rain

Former Rain

Anthologies (Editor)
Keeping the Faith
Have A Little Faith
This Far by Faith

EBOOKS
Love Isn't Enough
A Mighty Love
The Blessed One (Blessed and Highly Favored series)
The Wild One (Blessed and Highly Favored Series)
The Preacher's Choice (Blessed and Highly Favored Series)
The Politician's Wife (Blessed and Highly Favored Series)
The Playboy's Redemption (Blessed and Highly Favored Series)
Tears Fall at Night (Praise Him Anyhow Series)
Joy Comes in the Morning (Praise Him Anyhow Series)
A Forever Kind of Love (Praise Him Anyhow Series)
Ramsey's Praise (Praise Him Anyhow Series)
Escape to Love (Praise Him Anyhow Series)
Praise For Christmas (Praise Him Anyhow Series)

Prologue

The game was on, and Isaac Walker was at his plush 4,200 square foot suburban home relaxing as he watched the Charlotte Hornets play the Detroit Pistons. His sons, Donavan and Ikee, were in the media room with him. Before his wife, Nina, left for the movies with her daughter-in-law, she had made all their usual game day fare—Buffalo wings, popcorn, pizza, and spinach dip.

"I wish the food could just float over here to us," Donavan said. "These recliners feel so good I don't want to get up."

"Well, you'll starve if you don't get up. Because I don't care how comfortable these recliners are, they don't have special feeding powers." Isaac laughed at his son and then jumped out of his seat as his favorite basketball player did a lay-up over the head of another player.

"Since you're up, why don't you pass those chicken wings over here," Ikee said as he winked at Donavan.

"And hand me a slice of that deluxe pizza," Donavan added.

"You boys better be glad that I have mad love for you." Isaac walked over to the buffet table and made plates for his sons. He passed the plates over to them, and then made a plate for himself. As he was about to sit down, he heard a loud knock on the door. "Y'all hear that?"

Donavan shook his head as Ikee said, "I didn't hear anything."

"Someone is about to put a hole in the door with how hard they're banging."

As he made his way out of the basement, Isaac hollered, "I'm coming!", hoping that the banging would then stop. It did, but by the time he opened the front door he was surprised to see that no one was there. But the game was on so he wasn't going to waste precious time worrying about it.

He rushed back down to the basement and got comfortable in his recliner as he asked, "What did I miss?"

"Only some fancy foot work and the dunk of the year," Ikee told him.

"Wonderful!" Isaac was really ticked about the door incident now. Some impatient person, who couldn't wait the extra minute it took him to come upstairs to answer the door, made him miss what was sure to be an NBA highlight moment.

The Hornets had hot hands tonight. Everything they shot seemed to find its way to the basket. Threes, jumpers, lay-ups... no problem. The game was all good until the fourth quarter when the Hornets went to sleep and lost the game.

"What just happened?" Ikee asked as he stood up and threw his plate in the trash.

"I don't know, but if these guys want to make the playoffs, they are going to have to stop throwing the game away in the fourth quarter." Isaac shook his head.

"You need help cleaning up?" Donavan asked as he rose from his seat.

"Nah, I just might leave this stuff until morning, I hear my pillow calling me."

"Okay, but you know mama said that if she fixed the snacks she expected us to clean up behind ourselves."

"You let me worry about your mama." Isaac puffed out his chest like he was the man of the house and made the rules. It helped that he knew the housekeeper was scheduled to clean the house tomorrow morning.

He said goodnight to his sons. Donavan was headed home and Ikee was meeting some friends at a pizza joint to study for his SAT. The thought of Ikee studying for his college exams caused a smile to inch across Isaac's face as he closed the door behind his kids.

Isaac then made his way back down to the basement, deciding that he would at least throw the plates in the trash and wipe off the counter. The housekeeper could take care of the rest when she arrived in the morning. It only took a few minutes, and he was done and headed back up the stairs when somebody started banging on the back door as if he owed them money.

Ikee must have left his key. Isaac took his time getting to the back door. If Ikee was going to be a jerk about it, then Isaac didn't feel obligated to get his son out of the cold March wind any sooner than necessary.

He swung the back door open. "Boy, what is wrong with you?" Isaac questioned. He then noticed that he was yelling at the wind, because there was no one at his back door. Taking a quick look outside, Isaac figure some of the neighborhood kids were messing around. But just to be on the safe side, he turned on the alarm system before going to bed. If someone was out there trying to make trouble, he wanted the police to deal with them, rather than doing it himself. Isaac prayed that those days were over for him.

Isaac couldn't climb into his king-sized bed fast enough. The pillow-top mattress allowed him to sink into the mattress and drift right off to sleep. However, sleep didn't last long. A ringing in his head disturbed him. As Isaac tossed and turned he wondered if the telephone was ringing, but he couldn't reach out to get it.

Then he heard a sound, and knew instantly what was happening to him—he was receiving another visitation. Isaac prayed that this one was from God or one of His heavenly angels.

"Why won't you let Me in?" the voice asked.

Isaac told Him, "I tried, but no one was at the door."

"What door?"

"The front and back door."

"What about the door to your heart?"

"Huh?" Isaac was dumbfounded. He felt at peace as he conversed with whoever was invading his head tonight. He knew that this intruder was no intruder at all. It was his heavenly Father. Isaac was puzzled by the question, because God already had his heart.

"Follow Me," the voice commanded.

Isaac didn't even think to question the command. He hopped out of bed and was instantly transported from the suburbs into the heart of the ghetto. His eyes blurred with unshed tears as he witnessed murders, robberies, and drugs being sold and used while lives were being ruined in the process.

Iron bars were affixed to the windows of many small homes as if the people had become prisoners to the place they laid their heads. As zombie-like characters roamed the streets with no apparent destination, Isaac felt bile rising from the pit of his stomach as he realized exactly where he was standing.

"Doesn't look too promising now, does it?"

Isaac asked the man, "Why did you bring me here?"

"You used to call this place The Promised Land."

Looking around, Isaac wondered how he could have ever thought a place like this could be anything but the desolate place it now was. But back in the day, he and his partner-in-crime and best friend, Keith, thought they ruled these streets and that everything had turned up like roses for them. They never realized the stench that their illegal operation would eventually leave behind.

"Doesn't look very promising, does it?" The man repeated.

Isaac shook his head. He was too ashamed to say anything because he had played a part in the destruction of this community. What could he say? He certainly couldn't blame the people in the community like the media does. Isaac knew firsthand that hopelessness had brought on the ills that this community now suffered through.

As if being frozen in time, everything stopped. There was no movement on the streets; the people appeared frozen and even the wind stopped blowing. Then, Isaac heard the voice of his Lord ask, "Do you love Me?"

Isaac fell to his knees as the sound of his Lord and Savior's question penetrated his ears. He was confused= because he had been serving the Lord for many years. Why would his Lord need to ask such a question? Had he not shown his love for the Father time and time again? "Yes Lord, You know that I love You."

"Then feed My sheep." After saying those words, the Lord disappeared.

Isaac's eyes popped open. He was no longer in the heart of the ghetto. He was once again lying in his comfortable bed in a part of town where crime caught its residents off-guard because no one expected anyone to do them harm. But Isaac knew firsthand that the people who lived on the street he'd just been standing on were on high alert at all times, because predators walked the streets 24/7.

His Lord was asking him to come out of his place of comfort and do something meaningful about it. But what? He held a revival on the west side of town last year and hundreds of people gave their lives to the Lord. What else could he do that would really shake the place up and bring about a change?

As he pondered the situation, Nina opened the bedroom door and kissed him on the mouth. "Did you and your sons enjoy the game?"

"It was all good, until the fourth quarter. As usual," he complained.

"Why don't you just choose another team?" Nina asked, while pulling a night gown out of her dresser and heading to the bathroom to take a quick shower before bed.

"It's not that simple, baby. You don't just bail out on your team when they're down. You hold on, keep rooting for them, and pray that they make the shot next time."

Nina gave him a raised eyebrow look as she went into the bathroom, letting him know, once again, that she didn't understand his obsession with basketball. There was another obsession he had that Nina didn't understand either. And he knew that it was not going to be easy to tell his woman that his journey in the Promised Land was not yet complete.

Chapter 1

"Girl, I don't know what's wrong with this man I'm married to," Nina complained to Elizabeth Underwood, her best friend. Actually, the two women were not just best friends, they had been so close for over thirty years that they thought of themselves more as sisters than mere friends.

"What's he done now?" Elizabeth asked jokingly.

"What hasn't he done?" Nina was frustrated and didn't know what to do. "Here I am, planning Ikee's graduation party and helping him fill out his last few college applications, when my son tells me that he's not sure he wants to go to college right now."

"Did you pop him upside his head?"

"No, but I wanted to pop his daddy a good one." Nina shook her head.

Elizabeth laughed. "What does Isaac have to do with Ikee's not wanting to go to college?"

"Ikee has been helping his father with our new street ministry. So now, Ikee has gotten it into his head that he is being called into the ministry and he doesn't need to go to college."

"Did you remind him that Donavan was called into the ministry as well, but he went to college and so did Iona?"

"Thank you," Nina said to Elizabeth, as if she were preaching to the choir. "That boy thinks I'm boo-boo the fool or something. He's doing more than ministry on that street team. He's gotten himself involved with some girl and that's why his raggedy behind wants to stay. That's why I'm upset with Isaac. Because if he hadn't started this street team, Ikee probably wouldn't have met this little chicken-head girl and wouldn't be talking so crazy now."

"Nina," Elizabeth gasped. "That is so unlike you. I'm normally the one calling folks chicken-heads and rat-face or bone-head."

Sighing, Nina admitted, "I shouldn't have called that young girl anything but the name her mama gave her. But I don't even know what that is. Ikee keeps pretending that he hasn't a clue who I'm talking about when I ask about the girl he's dating. But he's not fooling me; I hear how he talks when he gets certain calls on his cell phone."

"You sound stressed."

"I am," Nina admitted. "When Ikee was born, I never thought that I would be pulling out my hair like this. But that stunt he pulled over a year ago that almost got him and his father killed still gives me chills. I've even had a few panic attacks when I've tried to help the street ministry."

"Did you tell Isaac about the panic attacks?"

"No, I've mostly just been avoiding the events. The spring and summer months don't last forever. I say, let them have their fun this year, and then we can go back to church inside the building that we built five years ago."

"Okay, but if the panic attacks don't stop, I think you need to seriously talk to Isaac and maybe see a doctor."

Laughing, Nina said, "The only doctor who can help me with my panic attacks would be a shrink and you know black folks don't go for that."

"What I know is that there are a bunch of crazy colored folks that need to rent space on some psychologist's couch. Matter-of-fact, renting ain't good enough; they need to buy the whole entire couch."

"Oh, so now you're calling me crazy."

"You're not crazy, but I do think you're stressed. I'm glad you called so we could talk this out."

"The person I really need to talk to is Isaac. But I don't know how to tell him to let go of a ministry he believes that God had commissioned. And for that matter, I don't know if I even should be feeling this way."

"You can't help the way you feel," Elizabeth said, with the compassion of a person who had been there, done that and would probably do it again.

"I know, but I feel awful for not whole-heartedly supporting my husband. I need God to move on my heart or change Isaac's."

"Sounds like we have a lot to pray about," Elizabeth told her.

"No doubt," Nina agreed. "But lately, I've been so stressed that I haven't been able to do much effectual, fervent praying, if you know what I mean."

"I got your back. Kenneth and I will be praying for your strength. But if you ask me, I think a girls' weekend is in order."

"Weekend? I need an entire week," Nina declared.

"Then let's plan something."

"Girl, I can't think about anything until this child of mine gets that diploma in his hand."

"I hear you," Elizabeth said. "But think about it. After Kenneth and I come up there for the graduation party, we are heading to Puerto Rico for a week. But after that, I'm available for any weekend, night... whatever you want to do."

"I don't know, Elizabeth. There's just so much to do around here. Isaac has big plans for the summer and he'd be disappointed if I wasn't here to help out."

"How are you going to help out when you're having panic attacks?" Elizabeth reminded her.

"I can make the flyers and help with some of the front end stuff."

"Sometimes, we women have to take care of ourselves. When Danae graduated from college, Kenneth and I took ourselves on a two-week cruise. It was wonderful. We turned our cell phones off and the only thing we concentrated on was relaxing. And guess what? The house didn't burn down while we were gone. The kids didn't go buck wild—at least not that we knew about."

Smiling at the thought, Nina changed the subject. "Enough about my crazy life, any more news about you becoming the next gospel singing reality TV star?"

"No news to give, I haven't talked to Kenneth yet, so I can't give the studio execs an answer one way or another."

"So, I'm not the only one avoiding important conversations with my husband," Nina chided her friend.

"I know, I know. But Kenneth is a very private man. He's dedicated to God, his family, and his ministry at the homeless shelter, but he has no patience for anything that might negatively affect either."

"And you think the reality show might become negative?"

Elizabeth giggled at that. "Have you seen the Mary Mary reality show? It's a train wreck, but I can't stop watching."

"I see your point. You might want to back away from that."

"But this could be really big for my career," Elizabeth whined.

"Then do it," Nina encouraged.

But, like a double-minded woman, Elizabeth said,"I don't think Kenneth is going to say yes. Then what do I do?"

"You keep your marriage intact and walk away from the reality show."

"Easy for you to say, Nina Walker. Your latest book is on the New York Times bestseller's list."

Elizabeth's sales had slipped in recent years, but she was still a bestselling artist. But Nina understood her friend's desire to get back some of the glory of her earlier days. "You're in a tough spot, my friend."

"Tell me about it."

"I guess I know what to pray about on your end," Nina told Elizabeth, before the two said their goodbyes.

Nina went back to work, outlining the novel she was about to begin writing. She should have started the novel a month ago, but things had been so chaotic that she hadn't been able to focus. Nina hated not meeting deadlines but with the way things were going, she already figured that she would have to ask her publisher to push the release date back. It was unprofessional, but until she had some confirmation that her son was going to do the right thing, Nina couldn't focus long enough to write more than a few sentences at a time.

"Hey babe, how's it going?" Isaac asked as he came into her office. He stepped behind Nina's desk and kissed her, while pulling her out of her seat.

Nina untangled herself and sat back down. "I'm trying to work on this outline so I can get started on this book that is due to my publisher in a few months."

"Okay, I won't keep you away from your work. I just wanted to talk to you about something."

"I wanted to talk to you too." She swerved around in her seat. She wanted to give her husband her full attention because she desperately needed him to pay attention to what she was about to say. Maybe this would help ease her mind so she could stop being so mad at him.

"You first," Isaac said.

Her husband looked to be in a good mood. Nina was silently praying that he would really hear her this time. "Have you notice that Ikee—"

At that moment, Ikee burst into her office, eyes filled with excitement as he yelled, "Did Dad tell you? Did he tell you?"

Nina leaned back. She smiled at her son because the excitement in his eyes was contagious. "Your dad and I just started talking, so he hasn't had a chance to tell me anything yet. Why don't you tell me what's got you so hyped?" She knew that 'hyped' wasn't a word the cool kids used anymore, but it was as close as she could get.

"It's going down this summer, Mama. We are taking it to the streets in the ATL, Chi-town, North Carolina, and right here at home."

"I don't understand. What are you talking about? And when is all of this supposed to happen?"

"Right after I graduate. Dad is planning everything out, but the first street revival will be here a couple days after graduation."

The excitement in Ikee's eyes was no longer contagious, because Nina was finding herself completely unamused by the entire conversation. She turned to Isaac and said, "Do you really think this is the right time for all of this traveling?"

"You sound like I'm planning a vacation or something. This is for the ministry, Nina." Isaac didn't know what was bothering Nina, but she'd been holding something in for over a month now.

"Your son hasn't even decided on a college yet. Why can't you and Donavan handle these trips and leave Ikee out of it?" Her voice was rising, and even though she tried to stop it, she couldn't bring herself back to a place of peace. She was going to have this out with her wonderful husband once and for all.

Isaac tapped Ikee on the shoulder and nodded his head toward the door. "Your mom and I need to talk. Close the door on your way out."

Ikee started to say something, thought better of it, then left the room and closed the door as his father had asked him to do.

Isaac sat down on the love seat in Nina's home office. He patted the seat next to him. "Come join me."

Nina sat down next to her husband. She didn't say anything because she was trying to choose her words. She truly loved this man that she had been with since she was nineteen years old, but he was testing her patience.

"Now, I know that you believe in the ministry just as much, if not more, than any member of this family. So, I'm confused about why you're so upset about the revivals we're setting up in each of these cities."

"Isaac, my spirit and my soul rejoices over all the wonderful works you're doing for the kingdom of God. But I have to be honest with you... I'm terrified by some of it."

He pulled her into his arms and leaned back into the cushions of the love seat. "God protects us, Nina. You don't have to worry about me out on those streets."

"I know that God protects us, but people seem to come out of all walks of life looking to settle some type of grudge against you." She turned in his arm, looking him in the eye, seeing everything she loved about him, but everything that terrified her as well. "I also don't like what's been going on with Ikee lately."

"Our son is doing good. He's about to graduate from high school next week and he's finally got his mind on the ministry."

"He's got his mind on more than the ministry. Something is up with him and I'm going to find out what it is."

Isaac pulled his wife closer to him. "Stop worrying. Ikee has finally got his head on straight. I'll be watching out for him while we're on the road."

Shoving his shoulder, Nina said, "I'm more worried about you than I am about Ikee. You find trouble everywhere you go. I'm too stressed out and really don't know if I can handle these events you have planned for the summer. I thought you were just going to do a few local events. Now you want to travel the world and run into more people that you've ticked off."

He leaned his head close to hers and kissed her. Then Isaac admitted, "Asking you to marry me was the most selfish thing I've ever done. I knew that life with me wouldn't be easy for you, but I couldn't imagine how my life would be without you."

"I don't want you to imagine life without me, but I don't want to be forced to live the rest of my life without you simply because you feel compelled to keep going back to those streets."

Shaking his head, he told her, "It's not me, Nina. I wish I could turn my back and forget I ever knew anything about them streets. But God has decided this thing for us. So, I've got to keep going."

Pulling away from him, she folded her arms around her chest as she stood up. "But I don't have to keep on going."

"Come on, Nina. Don't be like this. If I would have thought for one moment that you'd object to this revival, then I would have talked to you about it ahead of time."

She lifted a hand, halting his explanations. "I mean it, Isaac. I'm tired and I'm stressed."

"What do you want from me, Nina. Just tell me and I'll do it. Because I can't take you walking around here in a foul mood like you've been for the past few weeks."

Even though she hated feeling this way, she knew exactly what she wanted. She closed her eyes, hoping that she would feel different once she looked at him again, but as she laid eyes on him again, nothing had changed. "I don't want to go on this crusade with you."

Chapter 2

"What's the word?" her agent asked, as Elizabeth had barely put the phone to her ear.

"Good morning to you also, Allen." In the seventies, Allen Stein had been one of the top R & B voices in the country. Every album he put out went gold. It seemed like he had it all, but after a night of drinking and doing drugs, he'd wrecked his car and paralyzed the woman in the passenger seat of his car. Allen spent five years in prison, then gave his life to the Lord and proceeded to become one of the best agents the gospel industry had ever known.

"Yeah, yeah, yeah. Good morning and all that. Now tell it to me straight. Are we going in the reality TV biz or not?"

He was also pushy and demanding as usual. "I didn't get a chance to talk to Kenneth about this yet—" she began.

Allen cut her off, "Don't you live in the same house with the man?"

"Yes, of course we live in the same house." Rubbing her eyebrows as they arched, Elizabeth said, "Look, I'll talk to him today. I've got to go." She hung up the phone, wishing that she'd never picked it up in the first place.

Her conversation with Nina had been joyous, but Allen had not been so nice. He hadn't even offered to pray for her like Nina had. It's times like these Elizabeth was grateful that she had someone like Nina in her life. They were both dealing with issues right now and Elizabeth hoped that she had helped Nina as much as Nina had helped her.

Bottom line, she needed to quit putting it off and talk to Kenneth already. The recording industry was getting tougher by the minute, with producers constantly approaching her about putting her family on display by doing a reality show. They wanted her to have her husband relive the most horrific time in his life by telling the viewers about how it felt to be in one of the twin towers when the buildings collapsed.

As a result of the 9/11 attacks, Kenneth had been knocked unconscious. When he awoke at the hospital, he had amnesia. He had not remembered his daughters or his wife. Those had been some painful years for Elizabeth, but she had moved heaven and earth to reclaim her place with the man she loved. She actually thought that their story would be a wonderful testament to how God could heal and deliver two broken people. Her agent and record producer thought so too. The only person she had to convince was Kenneth.

Elizabeth had taken her time talking to Kenneth about the idea of a reality show because she knew his stance on their past—it was better left where it was. Now that Kenneth was a new man in Christ, he wanted nothing to do with the old man who'd once proudly cheated on his wife. And Kenneth still had nightmares about the day the World Trade Center collapsed with him in it. He'd always told her that any interview he did with her could not include questions concerning the events of 9/11. But the attack had occurred over a decade ago; surely he was over it by now.

She hopped into her royal blue Jaguar and rode off so she could meet Kenneth at the homeless shelter he ran. That was another reason why Elizabeth worried that Kenneth wouldn't agree to do the reality show. The studio producer thought that she needed to visit the homeless shelter from time to time to show the viewing audience that rich people had hearts too. She just hoped that Kenneth wouldn't think she was putting the people in that shelter on display.

As she walked into the homeless shelter, she caught a glimpse of Kenneth kneeling on the floor, blowing up an inflatable mattress for the guest that would be staying over tonight. That was how Kenneth referred to the homeless people who slept at his shelter, as guests. He tried to make the place as homey as possible.

His assistant, a young girl fresh out of college with a young face and shapely body, walked over to him. She handed him some papers to sign. Kenneth took the pen, signed the pages, and went back to what he had been doing without even a double-take at the girl. But Elizabeth did notice how Taylor looked at her husband as she walked away from him—as if she wanted him to notice her. But Elizabeth wasn't worried; her man knew where home was and so did she.

He looked up and saw her standing there. The smile that lit his face let her know how much she meant to him. She loved this man and he loved her. Life hadn't always been this good for them though. She and Kenneth had gone through the worst part of their marriage before he'd even lost his memory and almost died in the 9/11 attacks. Their children were grown now and hadn't witnessed their parents cut a fool in many, many years, but there had been a time, and as her husband walked over to greet her with a kiss, her mind drifted back to the day when she thought their love had come to an end...

After church that Sunday, Elizabeth got out of her brother's car and, as the girls ran up the walkway, she actually began to hope that things would finally be different between her and Kenneth. Danae did more falling than running.

Elizabeth smiled. It was so cute to watch her. She put the key in the lock and tried to turn it. The key didn't fit.

That's strange. She looked at the key. "Mmmh, it's the right key." She shrugged her shoulders and put the key in the lock again. It still didn't work. Dread swept over her, the likes of which she had not known in many years. She rang the doorbell, no answer. She banged on the door and screamed, "Kenneth, I know you're in there. You better open this door."

Kenneth walked into the foyer and spoke through the window. "You don't live here anymore, Elizabeth. I told you that."

"You said you were moving in on Monday."

"The locksmith was available today."

Elizabeth balled her fist. "Oooh, Kenneth, you better open this door!"

"Leave my children here and go find yourself a place to stay," he told her as he pulled back the curtain.

Elizabeth was hot. She stomped up and down the pathway trying to figure out what to do about this situation. That's when she spotted the decorative red bricks. Bricks she'd laid around the flowerbed when their love was in full bloom. "You think you can just put me out of my own house, huh?" She grabbed one of the bricks and threw it through the bottom pane of the window.

Kenneth opened the front door and menacingly moved toward Elizabeth.

"Daddy... Daddy!" the girls screamed.

Kenneth ran past them as Elizabeth picked up her second brick. "You lunatic. Only a fool destroys her own property."

She shook the brick in her hand. "I don't live here anymore, remember?" She reared back, ready to send another brick sailing through the foyer window.

Kenneth grabbed her arm and pulled the brick out of her hand. "You are the most selfish woman I have ever met. God, I can't stand the sight of you!" He moved back, trying to put some distance between them. He'd grown-up believing that only weak men beat their women. His father told him that it was easy to smack a woman around, but a real man takes time to talk things over with his woman—help her understand why things are the way they are. Real men loved their wives into submission, rather than beating a 'yes sir' out of them.

His dad took a hard stance against men who beat their wives. He should have stood just as firm against extramarital affairs, of which he had many. When he was a kid, Kenneth vowed never to take the easy way out. He would never beat or cheat on his wife. He had already broken one of his vows, now this woman was making him rethink the other. Kenneth wanted to smack the taste out of her mouth, but he didn't want to stop there. He wanted to keep on pounding until she was dead. Distance, that's what he needed.

Sirens could be heard far off.

"Don't you walk away from me." She strutted up to him and put her finger in his face. "I bet you feel like a big man today, don't you? Put your wife and defenseless kids out on the street with no place to go."

Sirens were blaring on their street.

"Get out of my face, Elizabeth." More distance, that's what he needed. But Elizabeth grabbed his arm. Her hand balled into a fist and she hit Kenneth in the mouth.

Erin and Danae were sitting on the steps crying. That's it, he'd had enough. Kenneth stepped back and raised his fist to retaliate.

"Don't do it, sir."

A White, heavy-set police officer approached as Elizabeth advanced on Kenneth like a tiger. Her claws dug into his skin. "Ouch!" Kenneth screamed.

The police officer grabbed Elizabeth and pulled her off of Kenneth. "Sir, we received a call about a domestic disturbance. Is this your wife?" he asked Kenneth as he held Elizabeth's struggling form.

"Let me go!" Elizabeth screamed.

Kenneth nursed the scratches on his face. "She's my wife."

"Do you want to press charges, sir?"

Kenneth watched Elizabeth struggle to free herself. Her eyes were ablaze with fury. He turned toward his children. They were huddled up together on the porch, crying their eyes out. "No, I don't want to press charges. I just want her off my property."

"Off your property?" Elizabeth broke free from the officer and lunged at Kenneth.

The police officer regained his hold on Elizabeth. "That's it. You're going to take a little ride with me." He took his cuffs out and put them on Elizabeth.

"No!" Erin shouted and ran to her mother's aid. She grabbed hold of Elizabeth's waist. "Leave my mama alone."

"Officer," Kenneth lifted his hands, "please... I'm not pressing charges."

"You two are disturbing the peace. One of you has got to go." The officer looked at Elizabeth. "Since this one appears to have anger problems, she should be the one to go."

Erin ran to Kenneth and pleaded, "Don't let him take Mama, Daddy."

The officer started walking to his car, dragging Elizabeth with him. She was huffing and puffing all the way. Kenneth sat Erin down on the porch and ran after them. "Look," he said to the officer, "this is the first time you've ever come out to our house. My wife and I lead a normal life, we've just been having a few problems lately." Kenneth couldn't tell if he was getting through to the officer or not, but he continued anyway. "Man, don't do this." He pointed toward Erin and Danae. "My kids... they don't deserve this."

The officer stopped and looked back at the tear-stained faces of the little girls on the porch. He let out a heavy sigh. "Okay, but if I let her go, you've got to get her into some anger management classes."

He looked at Elizabeth. She was practically foaming at the mouth. He didn't know how he would get her inside, let alone to anger management classes, but he would say anything to minimize the drama for his children. "Will do."

The officer unlocked the cuffs, took them off Elizabeth, and then turned her around to face him. "If I get another call about a disturbance at this house, I'm taking you to jail. Do you understand?"

She rubbed her wrist and nodded her head. "I understand."

"Good." The officer left and the Underwood family walked inside the house. Kenneth went to get the broom and dustpan to clean up the mess from the broken window.

Elizabeth was tired and weary from the struggle. She stood with her back against the door, holding on to the knob.

Kenneth started sweeping up the glass. Erin and Danae ran to him. Erin, the spokesperson for the duo said, "Daddy, please don't put Mama out. She didn't mean to break the window."

Kenneth moved his girls away from the glass. "Go play. I need to clean this mess up." Kenneth watched his girls run into the family room and sit in the entryway, peeking into the

30

foyer. He turned his cold, unyielding eyes on Elizabeth and whispered, "You take the master suite. I'll sleep in one of the guest rooms."

She rolled her eyes. "Your generosity overwhelms me."

"I'm not being generous to you." Kenneth peered around the corner and saw that Erin and Danae had scooted into the hall. "My children have been through enough. Just find a place to stay, Liz. I'll pay for it until you can get on your feet."

"Oh, you'll be paying long after I'm on my feet."

He kept his voice low, but his tone held purpose. "I don't care, Liz. Whatever it takes to get rid of you, I'm willing to do it."

"Who do you think you are?" She pushed herself off the door and got in his face again.

"Lower your voice."

She looked into the hallway and saw Erin watching her. She turned back to Kenneth and whispered, "I made you. Without me, you'd still be in middle management—somewhere being told what to do and when to do it. But look at you." She waved her hand up and down his physique and sneered, "Mr. CEO, top dog. You think you've gotten big enough to forget the bridge that carried your country-behind over?"

"Liz, I'm not going to tell you again, you need to back off of me."

Elizabeth was not intimidated. She pointed her index finger in his face. "If you think I'm going to let another woman come in here and enjoy the fruits of my labor, you've got another thing coming."

A bitter laugh escaped his lips. "If you think I'm divorcing you so I can have another woman, you're crazier than I thought." He sat the broom and dustpan against the wall and stood to his full height. He looked down on Elizabeth. "You, my dear wife, have cursed the institution of marriage. It'll be a long time before I can even think about putting a ring on a woman's finger without vomiting." He turned away from her and walked into the kitchen.

Elizabeth screamed at his departing form. "If you hadn't cheated on me, we—"

Kenneth turned on her. "I guess everything didn't go the way you planned it after all. Must've been a real shock to your system when you realized that I don't need you to survive, huh?"

No, Elizabeth hadn't figured on a lot of things back then. She was only grateful that the grace of God had allowed her and Kenneth to grow up and restore their marriage back to what God had intended it to be. Could she really put all they had built over the years in jeopardy, just so she could sell a few more CDs?

"I need to talk to you about something that's has come up. Do you have a minute?"

"For you?" He gave her a wry kind of smile. "I bet I could squeeze in at least two."

Chapter 3

Isaac and Keith clasped hands, then hugged. They hadn't seen each other in over a year and the pain of that absence was etched on their faces. "Man, the last time I saw you, you were on the mend from open-heart surgery." Pure joy exuded from Isaac's entire being at seeing his friend among the living. They had been through so much together, and Isaac didn't know what he would have done if he'd had to watch Keith being lowered into the ground.

Yeah, he understood that death would one day come for both of them and they would enjoy worship and fellowship with their heavenly Father, but he wanted to ride this thing out a little while longer with his boo and them rock-head kids.

"You're a sight for these old eyes as well," Keith told Isaac, with just as much joy in his heart. "It was close there for a minute, but I never stopped believing. Cynda kept telling me that God still had use for me on the mission field." Lifting his hands heavenward, he added, "I told the Lord that if He could still use me, then I was available."

"And I know for a fact that the Lord has use for you, because He has given me an assignment that I can't possibly complete alone."

Keith nodded. "That's all Cynda and I talked about as we drove down here for Ikee's graduation. Our boys are grown and thriving in their careers so Cynda and I have decided to move back here so that we can be right in the thick of things with you and Nina."

Isaac almost told Keith that he wasn't sure if Nina was interested in being in the thick of things with him anymore, but he held his tongue. God was well able to make things right with Nina, so he was just going to trust God to do His job. "I can't believe that you're leaving Chicago. All I can say is, God just answered one of my prayers, bro." They clasped hands again and then joined Nina and Cynda in the family room.

"What are you two grinning about?" Nina, Cynda, and Iona were seated on the sectional. Nina held Judah, Iona's first-born son, and Cynda held Joseph, the baby boy.

Cynda was Iona's mother and technically the grandmother of both boys. However, since Isaac and Cynda had dated many years before and conceived Iona together, Nina was the step grandmother. Iona loved both Cynda and Nina equally and thought of both women as her mothers. Few people could be so blessed to have two loving mothers when so many didn't even have one that they could count on.

Isaac had his arm on Keith's shoulder; the two men had become so in sync with each other that they looked more like brothers than friends. "Keith just told me that he and Cynda are moving back here to help with our street ministry."

Nina's mouth hung slack as she gave Isaac a dumb-founded stare.

"What did I say?" Isaac asked, clueless as to why his wife appeared so puzzled.

"Well, first I thought this street ministry was only going to be a local thing. Then you informed me of some plan to tour the nation with your street revivals this summer... okay, I accepted that. But if Keith is moving here to help with this street ministry, then this sounds permanent to me, and I'm just wondering when we will go back to simply ministering in the church that we spent all that money to build five years ago?"

"Baby, I don't know why you keep thinking of our street ministry as temporary. We discussed this when I was in the hospital, remember?"

"Which conversation are you referring to, Isaac?" Nina handed Judah to Iona as she stood. "Did we have this conversation when you were in the hospital recovering after some thugs came to our house trying to kill you and Ikee? Or are you referring to the conversations we had when you were recovering from a bullet that a very disturbed young woman put in you because of the life you lead on the street? Or maybe we had this conversation when I was in the hospital recovering after another thug from your past tried to kill me and your first-born son, Donavan."

"You've made your point, Nina. Trouble does seem to follow me. But I never lied to you about who I was." Isaac didn't want this thing between him and Nina to play out in front of family like this. But she was bound and determined to be heard, so he was going to give her the floor. He sat down and asked her, "If I am not to continue with this street ministry, then can you please explain to me how I can serve God, but not do His will?"

Nina huffed, "Who is going to take care of the church that we built while you're consumed with this street ministry business?" She said 'street ministry' as if they were dirty words, then continued her assault. "You're not going to lay all of the work of the church at Donavan's feet. He has enough to handle with the youth ministry and he has a family who needs him at home."

"If this is God's will for us, then everything will work itself out. Just relax, Nina, you're stressing yourself out needlessly." Isaac was saddened by Nina's strong objection to their street ministry. But he wasn't backing down… he couldn't. Not even for her.

Tears filled her eyes as she turned away from the group. "I need a moment," she said as she escaped to the safety of her prayer room.

Falling on her knees was not an uncommon thing for Nina, but falling on her knees to pray because she wanted to disobey a mandate from the Lord was something so foreign that she didn't know how to broach the subject with her Lord and Savior. How could she give an answer to such a thing? They lived to serve God—that had been an indisputable fact from the moment they got married. Was she now telling him not to serve God, or to only offer God whatever service she deemed appropriate?

Nina couldn't answer that, so she just let the tears flow and wished that Jesus was right there with her so she could wash his feet with her tears. But she was here by herself, and she had to deal with the nagging fear that something terrible would happen to her family if Isaac kept up with this street ministry.

"Lord, you know me," Nina said when she was finally able to speak. "I desire to do Your will and I don't like standing in the way of others as they do the will of God. But lately, I'm just afraid all the time. We are forever tormented by Isaac's past, and I don't understand that because You have cast our sins into the sea of forgetfulness and promised to remember them no more.

But all of Isaac's enemies sure seem to remember all of his past sins and they have made this family pay in ways that have simply devastated me. I know what I signed up for when I married Isaac, Lord, but I just didn't expect it to be this hard."

The door to her prayer room opened and Nina heard Isaac say, "Baby, can we talk?"

But she wasn't ready to talk yet.

~~~~

"If I didn't know you better, I'd think you were asking me to dredge up the most horrific time in my life just so you could sell a few more CDs."

"You're joking, right, Kenneth?" Elizabeth held her breath, praying that her husband would, just this once, do what was right for her. She had held off discussing this with him for as long as she could. But contracts needed to be signed and locations needed to be scouted out because there was no way that she was allowing cameras into her home on a regular basis. So today was D-day, and just as she thought, Kenneth was not in a cooperative mood.

"This is no laughing matter to me, Elizabeth. I'm not going to relive my past just because some reality show producer thinks our life together is too perfect and drama free. Guess what? I like it that way, we worked really hard for many years to get to this point, and now you just want to blow that all up?"

"I don't want to blow our marriage up, Kenneth. Don't be ridiculous. Only a fool would willingly tear down her own house."

He pointed at her as if to say 'ah-ha'. "But we were just that foolish when we were younger. Don't you remember my burnt clothes, and the two of us literally brawling over who would take the house, right in front of our kids? You might not mind reliving those times, but I don't ever want to see the man I used to be."

She heard her husband and even understood his point, but she was getting frustrated. "Kenneth, you're missing the point."

"And I can't believe those people want to bring cameras into our shelter. The people coming into this shelter need to be able to trust that we have their best interests at heart, and how much trust would they have after being exploited by some producer who is looking to create sensational television?"

Throwing up her hands, Elizabeth admitted, "I don't know what else to do, Kenneth. My CD sales are lagging, so my producer thinks that my career needs the boost that reality TV can give it."

Kenneth got up from his desk and moved over to the window where Elizabeth stood gazing out of it as if something else she needed was out there. But she just didn't know how to get to it. "I know how important this is to you and what it would mean for your career, but I think we both need to take a step back and consider if this is the right move for us."

"I feel like I'm losing ground," Elizabeth told him as she turned to face him.

Kenneth took her hand in his. "You are one of the top gospel artists in this nation. How on earth could you possibly lose ground just because you pass on a reality television project?"

"Open your eyes, Kenneth. I haven't been a top anything in the last three years. I'm happy for Tamela Mann and all the other gospel artists who are having great success right now, but I don't want their success to cause me to fade away."

Shaking his head, Kenneth told her, "I can't believe the words that are coming out of your mouth. You began singing gospel music for whom?" He put a hand around his ear, waiting on her response.

"For God," she admitted.

"So what if another gospel artist sells more CDs than you? Does that take away from the fact that you sing to honor God?"

Elizabeth had been told time and time again that her voice was made for gospel music because it was angelic. They'd told her that when she opened her mouth to give God praise, a hush fell over Heaven as God Himself listened to the sweet music as it drifted up to glory. Even though she understood that God wasn't judging her based on sales numbers like the record executives did constantly, something within her still desired to get back on top and be that number one bestselling, Grammy award-winning gospel artist again. So, needless to say, her wonderful husband didn't seem so wonderful at the moment.

Chapter 4

Isaac and Keith were at the church in the office making preparations for the street revival. Isaac hadn't anticipated Nina objecting to the street ministry on the basis that it would affect the work of the church's already established ministries. But the way he saw it, Keith couldn't have come at a better time because he was now the official director of the street ministry.

The two men shook on it, and then Keith said, "I never thought I'd be working for you again, my friend."

Isaac laughed at that. "At least this time we're working in a legal enterprise."

"That it is... a most Holy and legal enterprise."

Just then, Isaac's secretary rang in to tell him that Calvin Jones wanted to speak with him. Calvin Jones was the head man-in-charge on the streets these days. There wasn't a deal that went down that Calvin didn't have his hand in or hadn't at least blessed, like some sort of honorary god-father.

"Send him in," Isaac said, then told Keith. "This one ain't no joke. Watch my back."

"As always," Keith said.

The door opened and Calvin walked in. He was thin and only about 5'9. For a kingpin, Calvin didn't look like much of a threat. But he wasn't a kingpin because of his brute, the man was smart; he should have been a doctor or on Wall Street making his paper. But he'd been born to some dope fiends who could barely feed themselves, let alone send some kids to college.

Isaac had been praying that Calvin would come out of the life before the Feds got tired of recording his conversations and filming his every move. He might be a kingpin in the street, but he'd be another man's girl behind those bars.

"Hey, Pastor Walker." Calvin was all smiles as he stepped up to Isaac and shook his hand.

Isaac wasn't fooled by the smile. Calvin might not be much of a fighter, but he was hot-headed and let his pistol fight his battles. "This is Minister Keith Williams," Isaac said, making the introductions.

Calvin turned to Keith with a grin that was almost too big for his baby face. "I finally meet the side kick who is just as legendary as the man himself." Calvin clasped hands with Keith. "Good to meet you."

"Likewise," Keith said, and then moved to the back of the room to wait and watch.

What can I do you for, young man?" Isaac asked.

"I'm not so young no more, Pastor. I turned thirty yesterday."

"Well praise the Lord. Not everyone in your line of work makes his thirtieth birthday."

"Don't I know it. I buried two of my brothers last year. I got one more left, and he just went to prison."

"I'm sorry to hear that. I lost a brother and many friends when I was in the life. So I know that kind of pain."

Calvin stepped back and looked Isaac over as he said, "You the only preacher I ever heard that talks so freely about being in the game."

Isaac shrugged. "It's a part of my past… can't do nothing about that, but my hope is that others will learn from my cautionary tale."

Keith was still leaning against the wall in the back of the room, watching the exchange and praying for the young man like he'd never felt the need to pray for any other hustler he'd come in contact with in recent years.

"What's so cautionary about it? You used to be the man. Didn't nobody mess with you. You had it just like I got it on these streets, and then you just walked away from it all. And you still living large."

Isaac shook his head. "No, young man, I'm living for God. That's it and that's all."

Calvin lifted a finger as if he'd just remembered something. "That's what I stopped by to talk to you about."

"Have a seat." Isaac pointed toward the lounging area of his office. He then turned to Keith. "Why don't you join us over here."

Keith nodded, then sat in the chair to Isaac's left.

Isaac smiled at his old friend. Even when Keith was his lieutenant, he had been a man of few words, preferring to listen and observe. This ability of Keith's had saved Isaac's neck more than once, so he let the man handle his business in the manner he saw fit.

"Listen Pastor," Calvin began, once they were all seated. "I'm not here to tell you your business. But ain't nobody interested in your little street ministry because you're not meeting us where we're at."

Isaac leaned back in his seat and looked over at Keith to make sure he heard what Isaac was hearing. Keith nodded. If Calvin had come here to get Isaac to stop pulling souls out of the pits of Hell, then he wasn't going to be happy today.

"No disrespect to you, my granddaddy was a preacher and I loved that man like he was my daddy. He taught me to respect men of the cloth, 'cause he took care of me and my brothers while my mama was strung out and running the streets."

Okay, maybe Calvin didn't come here to cause trouble. Maybe the young-un had something to say that Isaac needed to listen to. "So, what am I missing?"

"The people who talk to me on them streets everyday," Calvin pointed toward the window, indicating the streets beyond the church, "they ain't tryin' to hear none of that 'peace be still' stuff you be preaching. Too many of our family and friends getting gunned down in the streets.And the messed up part about it is," Calvin stood up, getting animated with the flapping of his arms, "if we ain't out there killing our own brothers and sisters, then the police is doing it for us."

"Don't you think I know that folks around here are just waiting on a chance to go off? That's why I'm preaching," Isaac imitated Calvin, "that 'peace be still stuff'."

"Ain't nobody tryin' to hear that." Calvin threw up his hands. "Look, I'm only here out of respect. Word on the street is that you've got another one of your street revivals planned for next weekend."

Isaac nodded.

"I'm just here to serve notice that you might want to rethink that date."

"What's wrong with our date?" Isaac asked, not understanding.

"Let's just say that we about to extract some street justice for all of our brothers killed by the police, and we don't need this revival of your to steal our thunder... Ya feel me?"

Keith sucked his teeth as he joined the conversation. "What kind of street justice are you talking about?"

"I can't give away all our secrets… let's just say we about to take back our city."

"I hope you don't think that getting into a shoot-out with the police is going to make things better for the people in this community."

Calvin shrugged his shoulders. "If the police don't start none, won't be none."

"Just what are you planning to do, Young Blood?" Keith stepped to Calvin as he added, "Tensions between black people and the police are stretched thin as it is. But if you cause trouble, innocent lives could be destroyed."

"That's not my concern. And in case you haven't noticed, innocent lives are already being destroyed. Did Michael Brown have a weapon when that cop shot him down like a dog? What about Walter Scott over there in South Carolina? They had that man on film running when that cop shot him in the back. And I guess Freddie Gray asked those pigs in Baltimore to break his spine?"

Isaac understood the anger that so many people were feeling. He had much anger built up inside about those incidents as well. But, Isaac had channeled his anger into something productive—trying to help get these kids off the streets and change their mindsets so they aren't police targets in the first place. But based on the hatred Isaac saw in Calvin's eyes as he talked about the dead black men at the hands of the police, he knew Calvin's method of 'taking back the city' would not bring anything but more bloodshed and destruction. "This ain't gon' be good, Calvin. You might want to rethink this whole thing."

Calvin got out of his seat, a look of defiance on his face. "Ain't nothing in my life never been all good. Sometimes you got to take the good with the bad, and I might as well put Dayton back on the map while I'm at it."

"And you think what happened after Freddy Gray's death put Baltimore on the map?" Keith asked.

"Dang right it did," Calvin bobbed his head, clearly proud of what occurred in Baltimore, as if it was something akin to the March on Selma.

Shaking his head, Keith stood up, walked over to the door and opened it. "Thanks for coming by, we appreciate the heads up."

"So, what's up?" Calvin turned to Isaac. "You gon' cancel your revival or what?"

Isaac shrugged as he pointed toward Keith. "Keith manages our street team, so you'll have to talk to him about that."

Calvin stepped to Keith as if he had a beef to settle. "So I guess you gon' play tough and get in my way while I'm trying to do something to wake the people in this community up?"

"If you want to do something for the community, why not join forces with us and help out with this street revival?"

Calvin laughed in Keith's face. "I'm not on all of that Jesus stuff. You can preach that non-sense all you want, but count me out. I got too much money in my pocket to ever need Jesus or any of his disciples either."

"I guess that respect for preachers just went out the door," Keith said as the young man approached.

Calvin was angry; he wasn't used to being defied. "I gave you respect by even coming here. But y'all don't want to listen, got some death wish." He pushed past Keith, "That's on y'all, not me."

Keith closed the door behind Calvin, then he and Isaac shook their heads at the folly of the young man.

Pointing towards the door, Isaac said, "We used to be just like him. Only I didn't have respect for anything church related."

"Neither does he."

"He thinks he respects the cloth. But I've got a feeling that the life he's lead has caused him not to trust God." Isaac knew what that was like, because after watching his father kill his mother, Isaac had been ready to curse God to His face and take the consequences.

"And now here we come with this 'peace be still' stuff. How in the world do we expect people like Calvin to listen to a word we have to say next weekend?" Keith looked concerned.

But Isaac threw it back in his lap. "You're the one who told Calvin we weren't backing down, so you'll just have to figure something out."

~~~~

"You're coming to my graduation, right?" Ikee looked into Marissa Allen's eyes, daring her to refuse him.

"I don't think that's a good idea, Ikee. Your family will be there and they are bound to have questions about our relationship."

"That's why I want you there. I'm walking across that stage next week to make my mama proud. It's going to be the most important day of my life as far as my parents are concerned, so I want you there with me."

46

"Don't you think it will ruin the moment for your parents when they see me?" She patted her extended, rounded, stomach to drive the point home.

Ikee smiled at Marissa as he rubbed her stomach. He didn't care that she was seventeen and pregnant. He didn't care that she dropped out of high school a few months shy of graduation. A lot of kids in the neighborhood she grew up in did the same thing, they didn't see a future past the moment they were living in, so getting that piece of paper certifying completion of something meant next to nothing to them.

But Ikee knew that Marissa had a future. She was worth more than what others thought of her. And not just because of her beauty. Although, he freely admitted that her deep brown eyes had been the first thing he noticed. He then noticed the high cheek bones and buttery coated skin that seemed so silky and smooth that Ikee couldn't help but run his hand along her jaw bone, like he was doing now. "It would ruin the moment for me, if you don't show up. I need you there."

"But your parents..."

"My parents aren't nearly as scary as people think they are. Well, my father is, but my mother is a sweetheart. She will absolutely love you." He leaned forward and planted a kiss on her soft, supple, lips.

When their lips parted, Marissa stared at Ikee as if he had been sent down from Heaven, wrapped in a bow, just for her. "Are you sure?"

"Positive."

"Then I'll be there, baby."

"Good, now that we've settled that, come sit over here and tell me about your day." Ikee pulled Marissa into his arms as they sat on the worn sofa in her mother's small house.

"You always ask me about my day. And I keep telling you that I haven't done nothing but sit around here, watching TV and eating all the food in the house."

"What did you watch on TV?" Ikee asked, as if the answer was really important to him.

She looked at him for a moment as if she was trying to figure out if he was just trying to be polite. "You really want to know?"

"Marissa, how many times have I told you I want to know everything about you. You're my girl, and I like hearing the sound of your voice, okay? So, talk already."

Giggling, she told him, "Okay, but I'm as boring as they come. I do the same thing every day. But the highlight of my mornings is when I watch Creflo Dollar."

"See, right there, you and my mom have something in common. She loves Creflo Dollar and records his messages so she can play them back in the evening when she's done working."

"Well, we don't have that 'work' thing in common," Marissa said with a sadness in her eyes that was almost too painful to behold. "I don't have a job, I'm not in school. I'm nothing and your parents will see that and hate me on the spot."

Ikee tried to pull Marissa closer so he could take away all the sadness. But she pulled away from him.

"No Ikee, you can't make this better. I'm a complete screw up." Touching her belly she added, "I even managed to screw this up."

Ikee went to her. "Don't say that. How can you be a complete screw up if you're the best thing that's ever happened to me?"

She leaned into him and, as their foreheads touched, a deep sigh escaped her lips. She wanted to stay connected to Ikee for the rest of her life, but she couldn't just be some scrub who was dragging him down, causing him not to reach his highest heights. And she needed to figure out what she was going to do after she had this baby.

So, as bravely as she could, she put her hands on Ikee's face and looked at him for a long moment. Then she told him, "You have to leave. I've got a lot of thinking to do. And I need to be by myself to sort out some things."

He started to object to being thrown out when all he'd wanted to do was make her feel better, but he didn't want to upset her. "Okay, tell you what. I'll be back tomorrow and then you and I are going to have a serious talk."

She kissed him, letting him know that she had much love for him. Then she let him go.

As Ikee stepped outside and began walking toward his car, he noticed that the Range Rover parked behind his car was the same black-on-black as his daddy's. Then the door to the Range Rover opened and he saw it was his dad. Ikee's eyes bucked out of his head. "You followed me?"

Without even the slightest hint of concern about his actions, Isaac shrugged and told his son, "Your mom is worried about you. I had to figure out where you've been sneaking off to."

"I'm not sneaking anywhere."

Isaac leaned against his SUV and pointed toward the house. "Who's the girl, son?"

Ikee hesitated a moment too long. Isaac pushed off the SUV and headed toward the house.

Ikee got his voice back. He quickly said, "Marissa, okay? Her name is Marissa."

"That's a nice name." Isaac was now standing next to Ikee on Marissa's porch. He lifted his fist to knock on the door, but Ikee pulled him back.

"What are you doing?"

"I want to meet this girl."

"I already told you her name. Why do you need to meet her?"

"Why wouldn't you want me to meet her?" Isaac threw the question back at Ikee.

Ikee knew he wasn't going to convince his dad to just go back to his car and pretend like he hadn't seen what he thought he saw, so he simply said, "Okay, but before you go in, there's something you should know." Ikee's heart was beating so fast he thought it would come out of his chest. But then he man'd up and said, "She's pregnant."

Chapter 5

Graduation weekend finally arrived. Elizabeth and Kenneth were all packed and headed to the airport for Ikee's big day. They brought extra luggage because they were taking a week-long vacation in Puerto Rico before coming back home.

As Kenneth drove them to the airport, Elizabeth's cell phone rang. She was tempted to not answer it because it was her agent and she still didn't have an answer for him. But then she decided to be a woman about it and just face the awful music that was to come. "Hey Allen, I didn't think I would hear from you today."

"I know that you're on your way out of town, but this couldn't wait," Allen told her with grit in his voice.

"Kenneth is driving, so I can talk, at least until we get to the airport."

"I just received a call from the executives for the reality show. They love the idea we proposed, but they aren't willing to wait forever for you to sign the contract."

"I know this, Allen. But, I need some time on this."

"What's the problem? I thought you wanted this. You and I talked about how much this reality show could mean for your career, which could use a boost, in case you haven't noticed," Allen said, as if he was enlightening her.

Elizabeth had been number one on the gospel charts for so long that she thought it would always be so. But the last three singles barely made the Top 20 list. Kenneth told her not to worry. She was just in a slump and she would be back on top with her next release. But there were too many talented singers for Elizabeth not to worry. "I am very observant, Allen. So yes, I know that my numbers are down. It's just a little more complicated than I thought it would be."

"If that is code for 'your husband doesn't want to do the show', let me suggest that you explain the ins and outs of this business to the man."

Elizabeth side-eyed Kenneth as she said, "I can't discuss this right now. I'll call you back when we return from our vacation in about a week or so."

"That's not good enough, Elizabeth. If I don't have your contract back by next week, this ship has sailed." He hung up the phone.

She couldn't deal with this. Her children were grown and living their own lives. She didn't have any grandchildren yet, and Kenneth was always busy with the homeless shelter. What would she do if her career was suddenly over? Would she be content being the little woman at home again? Keeping the house clean and making dinners from scratch and waiting for him to come home to notice her? And would Kenneth then become the cheater he had been back when she was only a housewife?

"Allen still trying to pressure you to do that reality show?" Kenneth asked, pulling her out of her Betty Crocker/house-wife dream.

Kenneth was the man she'd married over twenty-five years ago and planned to spend the rest of her life with, but at this moment, she didn't even want to be in the same car with him.

"Allen is concerned about my career. He knows that this reality show will put me back on top. But you don't care anything about that."

"Whoa... hey, wait a minute." Kenneth lifted his right hand while steering the car with his left. "Who says I don't care about your career?"

"You don't have to say it, Kenneth. You're actions are speaking loud and clear."

As he pulled into the airport, Kenneth declared, "You've had a wonderful career. Everyone loves your music, even people who don't typically listen to gospel music love the songs you sing."

"Where have you been, Kenneth? My numbers have slipped so far that I'm not even a Top 10 artist anymore." She lifted a hand as he pulled into a parking spot. "Never mind, don't answer that, because I know where you've been—at your precious homeless shelter, worrying about them rather than trying to help me with my career."

Kenneth opened his mouth to respond to the allegations. But the words got stuck somewhere deep in his throat as he stared at his wife. He then opened the car door, stepped out, and pulled their luggage out of the trunk.

Refusing to be ignored, Elizabeth jumped out of the car and snatched her suitcase out of Kenneth's grip. "I'm right and you know it. That's why you have nothing to say."

As she attempted to walk toward the terminal with her luggage, Kenneth reached out and held onto her arm, causing her to turn back to face him. "I didn't say anything to you, because I finally realized how stressed you must be over your declining sales, and I would rather pray for you than attack you at a moment like this," Kenneth tried to explain.

But Elizabeth wasn't having it. "You could do a little less praying and a little more signing on the dotted line so we can get this reality show rolling, but you won't do that, will you?"

When he didn't answer, Elizabeth smirked, "I didn't think so."

~~~~

As Isaac walked into their bedroom, his mind was on Ikee and Marissa. Nina had been right to worry about Ikee's reasons for putting college on the back burner. Isaac had thought she was overreacting because his son was so dedicated to the ministry that he hadn't imagined anything else was pulling him away from college. Now he had to tell his wife what he'd just discovered, and he wasn't looking forward to this conversation. But Nina was already in an uproar about something else.

"Did you catch the news this afternoon?" Nina asked Isaac.

Isaac shook his head. "I've been too busy. I don't think I've watched the news in a few days." He strolled into their walk-in closet.

When he reappeared wearing a pair of pajama pants and white t-shirt, Nina told him, "Sounds like you need to cancel that revival. I don't think this is the right environment."

Isaac sat down on the bed next to his wife. "I'm not following, what has gotten you so worried?"

Rolling her eyes Heavenward, Nina felt like she needed to shake some sense into her husband's head. He just wasn't taking into account all the dangers associated with this taking-it-to-the-street type of revival he and Keith were putting together. "I know you're not crazy, Isaac Walker. You know there's trouble just as well as I know it. Especially since that

54

cop shot that boy in the back last week and those kids started rioting."

"I understand your concern about the riot. But that happened in Middletown, Nina. And it has nothing to do with what Keith and I are trying to do, except that we want to get these kids off the streets before any more of them die without having a chance to fulfill their purpose on Earth."

"That all sounds good, except for the fact that," Nina pointed toward the television, "they just reported on the news that a bunch of those same rioters are headed to Dayton to join forces with some of the local thugs here. They're going to loot and riot and make all kinds of trouble for people who had nothing to do with that shooting."

"That must be what Calvin had up his sleeve." Isaac shook his head.

"Who is Calvin?"

Isaac almost responded to the question, but then kept his mouth shut while staring at his wife a second too long.

His hesitation was noted. Nina hopped off the bed. "What aren't you telling me? What's going on?"

"Nina, calm down. You're getting excited over nothing."

She shook her head. "It's not over nothing. You knew about this riot before I mentioned it to you," she accused.

"I didn't know about the riot."

The nightly news had had ended so Nina changed the channel to CNN. They had reported about the Saint Louis and Baltimore riots, maybe she could get Isaac to listen to reason if CNN was reporting about a riot heading their way. But as she turned to the television, Nina wasn't confronted by news of any riots, but of something much more sinister and shocking.

Pictures of nine black men and women were displayed across the screen, and then the camera showed an image of a young, white man with an odd bowl-shaped haircut being handcuffed and led away. She and Isaac said nothing as they listened to the account of how this young, white man went into a black church in Charleston, SC, sat with the members of the congregation, and then took out a gun and began shooting. When it was over, he had murdered nine innocent people, who were guilty of nothing more than being black and worshiping the Lord at their church.

With a heavy heart, Nina turned to Isaac, a look of disbelief in her eyes as she asked, "How could something like this happen? Where was God?"

Isaac pulled his wife into his arms, trying to shelter her from her own doubts. As long as he'd known Nina, he'd never heard her question God about anything. She had been the one to teach him how to trust God no matter the situation. But isn't that one of the reasons man and woman join together in marriage—so that when one is weak the other will be strong? It was his turn to be strong in faith for Nina. Isaac wouldn't let her down.

"You're forgetting that God isn't the only player in this." Nina released Isaac as she wiped the tears from her face. Isaac continued, "Remember, baby, in these situations there is God, the Devil, and the rest of mankind."

"But isn't God all-knowing? Why isn't He stopping some of this stuff before it happens? I don't understand what's going on."

"I seriously believe that we are living in a Romans 1 kind of world. And that kind of world no longer hears God, they do what is right in their own eyes and they are filled with hate and murderous intentions."

"But in a church, where people were worshipping? I just don't get it."

"I'm amazed that you are even thinking this way, Nina. We've been in this way too long to not know what's really going on."

"I can't help it, Isaac. There is just too much tragedy going on in the world. I don't want to be, but I'm on edge all the time. Just last year, some thug came to our home trying to kill you and Ikee… now they're just going into the house of God and taking people out."

"Pull the Bible out of the drawer, Nina. I think you need to read Matthew 24:21-22 again. Maybe then you'll understand what we're up against and why it is so important for Christians to minister the gospel in whatever way the Lord leads."

"Just like you told me, there are more players than God in this. God could be leading people into certain ministries, or you could be leading yourself. And is God obligated to help if you came up with these street revivals all on your own?"

She was back to that. Isaac sighed as he tried to pull Nina back towards the bed. "Come sit back down so we can talk about this reasonably."

She shook him off. "I can hear what you have to say from right here. Who is Calvin?" She asked again, like a dog with a bone, refusing to let it go.

"Okay, you're upset. I get it. But Calvin Jones never told me he was going to start a riot here. I just assumed it must be him because he asked me and Keith to forgo the revival so he and his boys could do something about police brutality."

"And you didn't think to mention any of this to me?"

Isaac tried to laugh the matter off. "It's no big deal, Nina. We told Calvin that we weren't interested in helping with his crusade, because we had our own. End of story."

Pointing an accusatory finger at him, Nina shouted, "It's no big deal to you, Isaac Walker, because you're not afraid of anything or anybody. You think you're made of marshmallows and bullets just bounce right off of you. But I'm tired of dealing with these street thugs."

"Baby, you married a street thug," he reminded her, then instantly wished he hadn't.

Nina's hands went to her ears. "I don't care. I don't want to hear it."

Pulling her into his arms, Isaac told her, "I'm sorry, baby. I shouldn't have been so glib about it. I know that you have grown weary with the life you married into."

"Cancel it, Isaac. Cancel the street revival and I won't say another word about any of this."

"If I could cancel this event I would, just because of how upset you are… but this revival is bigger than both of us, Nina. This is my assignment from God."

Nina loved Isaac and she loved the Lord with all her heart. The last thing she wanted to do was come between anyone with an assignment from God. She stepped away from Isaac's embrace and went into their walk-in closet. When she came back into their bedroom she was carrying sheets, a blanket, and a pillow. She handed them to Isaac.

"So it's like that, huh?" he asked, looking a bit stunned.

"You have an assignment from God and I have a need to sleep all by myself."

After throwing Isaac out of their room, Nina did as he'd asked and opened her Bible to Matthews 24:21-22

For there shall be great tribulation, such as was not since the beginning of the world to this time, no nor ever shall be. And except those days should be shortened, there should no flesh be saved: but for the elect's sake those days shall be shortened.

Nina certainly felt like she was living in the day of great tribulation. You could hardly turn on the news without hearing about some tragedy to a family or a nation. Maybe she was getting a little weary with evil being at every corner. So if God was going to send the rapture to take her, the elect, away from this crazy and seriously messed up world, then all she could say was, come Lord Jesus.

Nina had been so stressed lately that she hadn't been picking up her Bible as much as she normally would have. So, instead of putting it down after reading the scripture Isaac had asked her to read, she turned to the book of Romans. As a writer, Nina loved reading the Old Testament because those pages were full of history and the emotions of life, but her husband had said that they were now living a Romans 1 existence.

She was now reading through chapter one of the book of Romans trying to see a resemblance to the world she lived in. The first several verses of Romans were filled with things that seemed rather ordinary and unrelated to the day they were living in. But once she got to verse 18, Nina began to remember what this chapter was all about…

For the wrath of God is revealed from heaven against all ungodliness and unrighteousness of men, who hold the truth in unrighteousness; because that which may be known of God is manifest in them; for God hath shewed it unto them.

For the invisible things of him from the creation of the world are clearly seen, being understood by the things that are made, even his eternal power and God-head; so they are without excuse: Because that, when they knew God, they glorified Him not as God, neither were thankful; but became vain in their imaginations, and their foolish heart was darkened.

Professing themselves to be wise, they became fools, and changed the glory of the un-corruptible God into an image made like to corruptible man...

Wherefore God also gave them up to uncleanness through the lusts of their own hearts, to dishonor their own bodies between themselves: Who changed the truth of God into a lie, and worshipped and served the creature more than the Creator, who is blessed forever. Amen...

And even as they did not like to retain God in their knowledge, God gave them over to a reprobate mind, to do those things which are not convenient; being filled with all unrighteousness, fornication, wickedness, covetousness, maliciousness; full of envy, murder, debate, deceit, malignity; whisperers, backbiters, haters of God, despiteful, proud, boasters, inventors of evil things, disobedient to parents, without understanding, covenant breakers, without natural affection, implacable unmerciful:

Who knowing the judgment of God, that they which commit such things are worthy of death, not only do the same, but have pleasure in them that do them.

As Nina closed her Bible, even though she was still upset with her husband, she had to admit that he was right—they were definitely living in a Romans 1 kind of world. She just didn't know what, if anything, she could do about it, and that terrified her.

Chapter 6

The next morning the Walker house was a flurry of activity. Iona and her husband Johnny were the first to arrive. But before Nina could close the door behind them, Donavan and his wife Diana pulled into the driveway.

As Donavan and Diana ran into the house, Nina said, "Well son, you came just in time to help me in the kitchen."

Donavan's eyes got big as he looked around the room, trying to figure out who his mother was talking to.

Diana laughed as she told Nina, "My husband only knows how to pick up the phone and order take-out if I don't get home in time to feed him." Shaking her head at Donavan, she told Nina, "But I'm here to help."

"Me too, Mama-Nina," Iona chimed in. "I didn't want you slaving away all by yourself this morning."

"Where are my wonderful grandchildren?" Nina asked Diana and Iona.

"Diana and I paid for a babysitter. Those kids lose their minds in public places. And don't nobody have time for that."

"I beg your pardon; my grandchildren are not that bad. They are perfect little angels."

"Speaking of perfect little angels," Johnny said, "where is our graduate?"

"Ikee has a big day ahead of him full of family and friends and, most importantly, getting that high school diploma that none of us thought he'd be getting this time last year." Nina took a deep breath and then exhaled, "So I'm letting him sleep in."

Iona and Diana followed Nina to the kitchen while Donavan and Johnny went to the family room and stretched out on the sectional. It was 7:30 in the morning. Nina planned to have breakfast on the table by nine so they could have fellowship, eat, and then get down to the convention center by noon for Ikee's graduation ceremony at one. "Daddy still asleep?" Iona asked while chopping up onions and green peppers for the omelets.

Nina was still so upset with her husband that she hadn't even gone to the guest room to check on him when she woke up. But knowing Isaac, he would be asleep for at least another hour. She wasn't about to get Iona involved in their argument, so she simply said, "Your daddy don't like to get out of bed before eight. He'll be down soon enough." Nina put her big iron skillet on the stove and started frying up a whole pack of turkey bacon. She was careful to keep her back towards Iona, so as not to give away any of the thoughts floating around in her head concerning Isaac.

But if Nina was truthful with herself, she would have to admit that the struggle with her husband and her discontentment had not begun with the planning of these street revivals. What she was feeling now began the first time she had visited Isaac in the hospital after he'd managed to get himself shot. Her husband lived a dangerous life; things really hadn't changed even after Isaac gave his life to the Lord because old enemies kept coming after him. Nina wanted them to run away from the evil and find their place of peace. But Isaac wasn't allowing that to happen with this street revival madness he came up with. These street revivals were keeping her family right in the mix with the same thugs who tried to kill her husband every other Sunday, or so it seemed.

But while Isaac hadn't changed much throughout the years, because he still had the lion's heart that wasn't afraid of anything and was always ready to take on any challenge that got in his way, Nina had changed. Every time some thug tried to take her husband's life, Isaac appeared to get stronger, but Nina had died a little each time. She was scared all the time these days and didn't know how to express that to Isaac or how to let God into fix what troubled her heart.

"The bacon is burning," Diana said as she nudged Nina.

"What? Huh?" Nina looked at the skillet. "Oh my goodness." She scooped the bacon out of the pan and then put on some sausage links.

Iona and Diana side-eyed each other. But before they could ask any questions there was a knock at the kitchen door.

Nina opened the door and greeted Keith and Cynda as they walked into the kitchen. "Good morning, good people," Nina said, as she hugged both of them.

"Good morning to you as well," Cynda said after she handed Nina a big pan of sausage gravy and biscuits. "My contribution to Ikee's graduation breakfast."

"You shouldn't have," Nina said.

But Iona grabbed the pan away from Nina, sat it on the table, and began examining the goodies. "Yes, she should have." Iona looked toward Cynda and said, "Mama, you know how I love your biscuits and gravy."

Nina and Iona had a special relationship, but it never bothered Nina when Cynda came around and she had to share her stepdaughter with the woman who gave birth to her and raised her for the first nine years of her life. "Well, in that case, thank you for bringing the biscuits and gravy. Hopefully, the rest of us will be able to get a little taste before Iona goes to town on it."

"Is Isaac up?" Keith asked.

Nina pointed upwards. "He's in the guest room. You can go on up."

Iona and Diana side-eyed each other again. But Nina kept working on her breakfast and paid them no mind.

Keith made his way upstairs and knocked on the door to the guest room.

Isaac said, "Come in."

Keith pushed the door open and stared at his friend for a moment before laughing in his face. "Since when did you become a guest in your own home?"

Isaac was sitting on the bench at the foot of the bed putting on his socks. He looked up at Keith and said, "Hand me those shoes next to the door, funny man." Isaac had already showered and dressed by the time Keith came up the stairs. After tossing and turning in the full size bed, while Nina probably slept peacefully on their king size, pillow-top mattress, Isaac decided to get up early this morning in order to take care of his problem.

Isaac put on his shoes, stood up, and grabbed his keys. He started walking toward the door, then turned back and asked, "You coming?"

"You can't go anywhere right now. Nina's down there cooking up a big breakfast for everyone."

"If I don't leave right now, I'll be in this guest room again tonight. And that just ain't happening."

~~~~~

"You ready to tell me what's going on?" Keith asked, as Isaac backed out of the driveway and headed down the street.

"I already told you... I need to see a man about my problem."

Keith shook his head. "I'm talking about you and Nina. You're sleeping in the guest room and she barely even looked your way as we left the house."

Sighing as he turned the corner, Isaac admitted, "She wants me to cancel the street revivals."

"That doesn't sound like Nina. She's always been down for the work of the ministry."

"She's changing, Keith. And I can't blame anyone other than myself for what Nina is going through. To top it all off, the one thing she wants from me, I can't give her because I'd be going against God."

"Nina's got to think long-term," Keith advised. "Because having you turn away from the Lord will not benefit your family when all is said and done."

"The problem is, she's not thinking long-term. The only thing she's thinking about is how dangerous this street revival could be, especially after hearing a report on the news about some riot that's been planned for this weekend."

"What riot? I didn't hear anything about a riot. Maybe Nina's thinking about what just happened in Middletown."

"No, she's right. Some idiots posted on Facebook about the riot. They plan to use our revival as their jumping off point. And I know whose idea that was."

They were driving through the hood as Keith asked, "You don't think that little weasel is getting this going, do you?"

"I know he is." Isaac pulled up to a trap house, turned off the engine, and opened the door. "You coming?" he asked Keith as he got out of the car.

"Boy, you know I've always had your back."

Calvin saw them coming and stepped onto the porch of the broken-down house he used for his drug trafficking. "You must be slipping in your old age, because all I've ever heard about the great Isaac Walker is that when he comes for you, you won't know you've been got until it's too late. But I spotted that Range Rover right off."

"I would have figured you'd still be asleep at eight o'clock in the morning," Keith said as he and Isaac stepped onto the porch.

"Naw man, I've always been an early riser. I like to catch the morning news. When I was a kid and my mom wouldn't come home at night, I would get up and check out the news. As long as they didn't mention her name, then I knew she was all right. Then one morning, these newscasters were standing in front of this van that had been set on fire with a man and a woman inside. I remembered thinking how sad it must be to have your life ended like that... then my granddaddy came to the apartment. He packed up our clothes and told me that my mama died in a fire. You'd think I'd stop watching the morning news after that... but I'm hooked."

"You're not the only one watching the news, Calvin." Isaac wasn't about to admit that it had been his wife who'd clued him in about the riot. So he just got in the man's face as he added, "I need you to shut this riot situation down."

Calvin laughed. "How can I shut down something that has already happened?"

"I'm not talking about the riot that just took place in Middletown. I'm talking about the one you're planning right here in Dayton, at the same time as our revival."

With a look of defiance on his face, Calvin barked, "Y'all didn't want to help the cause when I brought it to you, so y'all might want to back off my porch."

Steam was rising as Isaac's nostrils flared. Who did this little wanna-be-gangster think he was talking to? Isaac saw himself putting a death grip on Calvin's throat and squeezing until this parasite took his last breath. Just as he was about to make his fantasy a reality, Keith put a hand on his shoulder.

Then Calvin said, "Why are you here? You need a rock or something?"

Keith poked Calvin in the chest while still keeping a hand on Isaac's shoulder. "We came to let you know that this is not going down… not in this town, and not during the revival. You claimed that you respected preachers because of your granddaddy. So, respect that."

"Respect time is over. I did my part. Y'all didn't want to listen. So whatever happens, happens."

"I don't think you understand." Isaac's voice was lethal as he stepped closer to Calvin. "This town deserves better than the likes of you. You're only interested in promoting your brand of hate. But I'm not going to let you get away with this. So either get the message or deal with the consequences."

Calvin wasn't budging. Isaac may have been the man back in the day… but as far as Calvin was concerned, this was a new day and a new generation. He was the man now, and he was going to do just what he pleased. "You delivered your message. So, now you can be on your way."

As Isaac and Keith stepped off the porch and headed back to the car, Calvin called out to them. "Oh… and, pastor… I wouldn't come back here without being strapped."

Like a predator spotting his prey, Isaac swirled back around and got in Calvin's face. "I have never needed to be strapped to handle a little parasite like you. So, let me put it to you like it is."

Calvin gulped, but stood his ground as Isaac continued, "I'm not asking you not to cause any trouble for the people in this neighborhood, I'm telling you. Because all you pack is a gun, while all of Heaven backs me up, and believe, my help comes fully loaded and prepared to take care of business."

Chapter 7

"Oh my God, it has been ages since I've laid eyes on you." Nina hugged Elizabeth as if her best friend had been kidnapped and they had just gotten her back home. In reality the two talk on the phone all the time, but hadn't seen each other in person in the past five years.

"I love you too, girl. But let go... I can barely breathe."

Stepping back and letting go of her best friend, Nina smiled at her. "Sorry about that. I'm just so happy to see you." Tears cascaded down Nina's face as she said, "We have to stop letting so much time go by before we get together."

"I know," Elizabeth agreed, "but either I'm busy recording or you're busy writing that next bestseller. But we have got to stop letting things get in the way."

Nina hugged Elizabeth again, but this time not so tight. Then she moved on to Kenneth and gave him a big hug as well. "Get on in here so we can eat this breakfast."

The rest of the gang was already around the table with only two exceptions—Isaac and Keith. But Nina wasn't going to let that stop her from enjoying breakfast with family and friends on the morning of her youngest son's high school graduation.

"Where's Isaac?" Kenneth asked as he pulled up a chair for Elizabeth.

Nina wasn't even curious about her husband's whereabouts this morning. She still very much loved her man, but his presence was so all-consuming that she was enjoying the break from it right now. Shrugging her shoulders, she said, "I'm not sure where he went off to." She glanced at her watch. "But we've got to get to the convention center pretty soon, so he'll just have to eat leftovers when we get back."

"But Dad doesn't like leftovers," Ikee reminded Nina.

Nina ignored her son as she sat down, bowed her head, and prayed over the food. Just as they began passing the plates around, the kitchen door opened and Isaac and Keith strutted into the dining room as if they were the guests of honor for this breakfast.

"I'm back," Isaac proclaimed. "Glad I didn't miss the food."

"Since we had no idea when you'd be back, I didn't want to keep our guests waiting," Nina told him curtly.

"Good call," Isaac agreed as he placed a kiss on her cheek.

Nina couldn't stop herself from smiling at the show of affection. She loved her husband and nothing would ever change that, but some things had changed and Nina didn't know how to un-change them. Not this time.

Isaac and Keith joined them at the table. Nina smiled, laughed, and chatted, but she wasn't really in the moment. She just kept telling herself that today was the day her last child would graduate from high school. She would wait until tomorrow to start lobbying for college again. Because there was no way she was going to allow Ikee to work with his father all summer long with no thought as to what school he would be attending in the fall.

"Did you hear me, Nina?" Isaac called out to her.

"Huh? Oh, no, I'm sorry, Isaac. I didn't hear you."

Grinning at his wife's absent-mindedness, he repeated, "We'd better get going if we're going to get Ikee to his graduation on time."

She glanced at her watch. "Oh, yes, you're right. Let's get out of here so I can watch my son accept his diploma."

"I'm driving," Isaac told her. "You got up so early this morning to fix this wonderful breakfast that I think you're still a little sleepy."

~~~~

Isaac was behind the wheel and Ikee was in the back seat of the car. Nina was still in the house, so Isaac took this moment to have a heart-to-heart. He turned to his son. He didn't have much time because Nina would join them in the car soon, so he skipped the niceties and asked, "Are you sure this girl is right for you?"

"I know what you think, Dad. But I'm not only with Marissa because of the baby. It's not like that."

"That wasn't what I was thinking. What I'm wondering is if you're trying to help this girl because of Candy." When Ikee had gotten himself in trouble over a year ago, he had run into a crackhead named Candy. At first he had treated the girl badly, but later, as Ikee figured out that he wasn't cut out for gang banging and selling dope on street corners, he also realized that if he didn't help Candy, she would be dead soon. Once he got it in his mind that Candy needed his help, Ikee risked his own life in order to bring that girl out of the horrible life she had been living.

"What about Candy?"

"I'm just wondering if Marissa is another one of your crusades. Because if she is, you don't have to throw your life away. Your mother and I can help Marissa while you go on to college and live your life."

"I thought you were in agreement with me about putting college off for a while?"

"I was when I thought you were foregoing college because of the ministry. But not so you can stay here and play daddy to this girl's baby." Isaac shook his head like he wasn't about to let that happen.

"She's not a crusade, Dad. I really love Marissa."

Isaac took in his son's words and then asked, "Is the baby yours?"

"I'm going to treat it like it's mine."

Ikee was talking crazy, but Isaac didn't have time to set him straight because Nina was headed toward the car. "Don't do anything drastic before I can talk to your mother about this."

Hopping in the car, Nina gave both her men the brightest smile they'd seen on her face in weeks. "Let's get this party started," Nina said as she put her seat belt on.

"Yes ma'am." Isaac started backing the car out of the driveway, hating that he would soon be wiping that smile off of his wife's face.

"Hey Ma," Ikee called out to her. "After I get this piece of paper, Dad and I want to talk to you about something. Is it okay if we let the others go to the restaurant without us?"

"Sounds serious." The smile on Nina's face was fading as she gave Isaac a cold, angry stare.

Isaac didn't know what had gotten into his wife, but he wasn't about to keep taking all these angry stares and accusations from her. He was on a mission from God and Nina would have to accept that sooner or later.

"What's got you so upset?" Isaac asked, after Ikee jumped out of the car to catch up with a few friends as they were headed into the convention center.

Nina turned to Isaac. She put her head in her hands before answering, trying to calm the raging storm that was building inside of her. As she lifted her head to face Isaac, she didn't answer his question, but rather asked one, "Do you really think Ikee should delay going to college?"

Isaac wasn't going to bust Ikee out before the two of them had the chance to sit down and talk to Nina about this pregnant girl. So, he answered her question without incriminating himself. "I'm not sure if it's the right thing for Ikee or not," he admitted. "But I do know that every kid is not cut out for college."

"Donavan did well in college. Iona not only did well, she was on the Dean's list and went on to law school. Our kids are smart... they can take on any challenge that's put before them. I just don't understand why, after he and I sent out numerous college applications and stayed up late at night talking and praying about his options, he would suddenly decide that he's no longer interested."

"Kids do it all the time, Nina. Let's just roll with him on this one and see where it takes him. God may have a better plan for Ikee, so we don't want to stand in the way, right?"

Rolling her eyes to that non-sense, Nina told him, "That's easy for you to say. Ikee wants to join you all summer long. So, of course you're not going to stand in his way."

Someone knocked at the window. Nina turned to see Elizabeth waving at them. "Are y'all going to sit out here while the graduation ceremony is going on or what?"

Nina hopped out of the car and started walking with Elizabeth without waiting for Isaac to get out of the car. "Girl,

I'm so ready for this day, I'm not about to miss a minute of my son getting his diploma."

"You sound like me when Erin was graduating college. That girl stressed me out so bad her last two semesters that I wasn't sure if she would finish."

"You know my pain," Nina joked with Elizabeth. "Let's get in there and take a seat before this boy decides he doesn't even want this diploma."

While Cynda, Iona, and Diana walked in behind Nina and Elizabeth, the men stood by the car as Isaac looked as if he'd lost something and didn't know the first thing to do to get it back. He shook his head. "Well, I guess I'm still invited, seeing as I'm the father of the graduate and all."

Patting his friend's shoulder, Keith said, "She'll calm down, my friend. And then things will be back to normal."

"When?" Isaac asked, as if he desperately needed to know the timeline. "She's been on ten since Ikee told her he'd rather work with me in the ministry than go off to college."

"Then you've got your answer," Donavan said, grinning. "Just tell Ikee he has to go to college and Mom will stop being all—" Donavan lifted his hand as if it was getting ready to claw his dad's eyes out.

"Boy, don't tell me how to handle my woman." Isaac playfully gut punched his son.

"All right, old man. Don't start nothing you can't finish."

Isaac looked to Keith and said, "You better tell him, before I have to show him."

"You don't want none, Youngblood. I've seen your daddy finish plenty of what he started." Keith then pointed toward the convention center as he said, "The only person I've ever known your dad to have trouble handling just walked in that building over there."

"That's just it," Isaac answered, as the men began walking to catch up with their wives. "I haven't tried to handle Nina since we've been married. I let the good Lord deal with my wife."

"If all the shade Mom was throwing your way this morning is any indication, then I think you should get to praying," Donavan told him.

"Don't you worry, son... I've already got that covered."

~~~~

The graduation was beautiful. When Ikee stepped onto the podium to accept his diploma, Isaac and Nina high-fived each other and screamed, "We did it!"

That moment was the highlight of the day for Nina. And she hoped that just the simple act of touching his diploma would cause Ikee to think more seriously about college and his future. But those hopes were soon ripped to shreds. They stood outside getting ready to head to a restaurant to celebrate when a young woman ran up to Ikee, wrapped her arms around him and then kissed him as if his teeth were made of gold and she was trying to suck the fillings out.

Nina stepped forward and pulled the two apart. She stood between her son and this girl who'd just slobbered all over him in front of God, Ikee's family, and whoever else wanted to see this outrageous display. "What is going on here?" she asked Ikee. She then turned to the girl before her son could respond and asked, "And who are you?"

"Mama, Mama, it's cool," Ikee said nonchalantly. "This is my girl, Marissa."

"Marissa who? I've never met…" Nina was saying, but as her eyes traveled the length of the girl, she turned her head, in search of Isaac as she pointed to the bulging stomach in front of her. "Isaac, oh my God. This girl is pregnant."

Chapter 8

"Calm down, Nina. Let's sit down and talk about this."

"Don't you tell me to calm down, Isaac Walker." They were in their bedroom and Nina was wearing out the carpet, pacing back and forth. "I kept telling you something was up with this boy wanting to skip out on school, but you acted like I didn't know what I was talking about."

"I didn't say that," Isaac objected. "I just wanted to let Ikee make his own decisions... like a man."

"Oh, he's making grown-up, man-like decisions now... that's obvious after seeing that pregnant girl slobbering all over him." She threw a pillow at Isaac. "And you just stood there, letting your son behave like that."

"What do you want me to do, Nina? He turned eighteen two months ago. It's not like I can send him to his room or take away telephone privileges anymore."

"See what I mean?" She pointed an accusing finger at him. "Being eighteen doesn't mean he's a grown man. He's still very much a boy in many respects and that's why I'm putting my foot down. That girl is not getting her hooks into my baby."

"Your baby is eighteen."

"Will you stop saying that?" Nina screamed at him.

He didn't know how to make this one better for her. Ikee was in love with a pregnant girl and planning to help the girl take care of the baby. He didn't think Ikee was ready to take on the responsibility of a baby. But telling Ikee that would most likely cause him to want to be with this girl all the more.

"And why did you invite that girl to this house?" Nina was angry—angrier than she'd ever been at any point in her life. Her son's future was being snatched from him by some baby-mama and Nina wasn't having it.

"Because we need to sit down with Ikee and Marissa and find out where their heads are at." Isaac held out a hand for his wife and waited by the door for her to do the right thing.

Defiance was written all over her face as she folded her arms around her chest. "I don't want to talk to her."

Isaac held out his hand. "We don't have a choice, baby. We need to do this for Ikee."

Sighing deeply, she relented. Nina unfolded her arms, took her husband's hand and marched into the family room where Ikee and the very pregnant Marissa were waiting. The rest of the group had gone out to dinner in order to give them privacy. But Nina didn't want any private moments with Marissa. She wanted to hop on the next plane headed to some far, far away place where she could protect her son from girls like Marissa.

Isaac got the conversation started. He turned to Marissa and said, "First off, I'd like to welcome you to our home."

"Thank you so much, Pastor Isaac. My mama always said that you was real cool people. And when y'all did that revival in my neighborhood and Ikee came knocking on my door, I found out first-hand just how cool y'all are."

Nina's head almost snapped off her neck as she darted her eyes from Isaac to Ikee, then back to Marissa. "Are you telling me that you met my son while he was out doing work for his father's street revival?"

Grinning as she glanced over at Ikee, Marissa then quickly turned back to Nina. "Yes ma'am. Ikee was so sweet, coming to my door with those tracts talking about how God could save my soul." She laughed at the memory. "I told him that I didn't have time to worry about Heaven because I was too busy trying to survive from day-to-day right here on Earth."

Ikee joined in, "I gave her your favorite phrase, Mom… 'I wouldn't want to live or die without Christ in my life'."

Marissa's eyes got teary and Nina could see that those words had an impact on the girl.

Wiping a tear as it traveled down her face, Marissa said, "I had never heard anything like that before. Certainly no one in my family was thinking about living for God in the here and now. All we've ever been taught to do is scratch our way from the bottom, just to get barely above ground.

"But when Ikee told me that I shouldn't live or die without Christ in my life, it felt as if God had finally opened my eyes and I was able to see the truth. He led me in the sinner's prayer that day and came to see me at least once a week, if not more, since that time."

That was obvious, Nina thought. If the boy hadn't been sniffing around, then Marissa wouldn't be in their house looking for child support. "How many months are you?" Nina appreciated that Marissa had accepted the Lord into her life, but she couldn't understand why Ikee or Marissa were willfully having sex knowing that they were neither married, nor able to take care of a child.

"I'm almost seven months pregnant, ma'am," she answered respectfully.

"So you and Ikee must have met during the first revival we held over on Brown Street last year," Isaac said, trying to put the dates together.

"No sir, I don't live on Brown Street. I live on Riverview, remember?"

Nina glanced at her husband. Why was this girl asking him if he remembered the street she lived on? Isaac didn't know this girl.

"That's right," Isaac said quickly. "We had a revival on the corner of Riverview and Broadway in that abandoned lot."

Nina quickly counted backwards and then asked, "But wasn't that revival about five months ago?"

Isaac did a little math in his head and then he and Nina turned to Ikee at the same time. But it was Nina who asked, "How could you have impregnated this girl seven months ago, if the two of you hadn't even met yet."

Marissa stood, shaking her head. "I'm not pregnant by Ikee. I'm sorry if that's what you were thinking. But no, Ikee and I are in love with each other, that much is true. But he had nothing to do with getting me pregnant."

"Who is the father, if you don't mind us asking?" Isaac said.

"Some loser who wants nothing to do with me or the baby. I've tried my best to stay out of his way and he avoided me like the plague since the day he found out I was pregnant."

"Does he live in Dayton?"

Marissa nodded.

"Well, if you and Ikee are hanging out, then I think we should at least know this man's name." Nina didn't want any surprises. Not in this town; surprises got you killed.

"I understand why you would want to know all about me. But I'm really embarrassed about the situation I've put my child in, so I don't like talking about him, but if you really—"

Ikee jumped up. "You don't have to give us his name. Because once we're married, the baby will have my last name anyway."

"Married?" Isaac couldn't believe what he'd just heard.

"Yeah, dad. I already told you that I plan to treat Marissa's baby like it's mine. The only way I can do that is to marry her and give the baby my last name."

Nina swung around to face her husband. Her eyes were bulging out of her head as she asked, "You already talked to Ikee about this? You knew?"

"Yes, but we were going to tell you everything after graduation. That's what Ikee wanted to talk to you about today. But I had no idea that Marissa was going to show up at the graduation."

She was about to lose her mind. This wasn't happening. "And you kept this from me? How long have you know about them?"

"I just found out yesterday. You had been so worried about Ikee so I followed him, and that's when I found out what he'd been doing."

"But you didn't say a word to me about this last night."

"You had other things on your mind; I didn't think it was the right time to discuss this."

"You had no right to withhold this information from me. I'm his mother." She pointed at Ikee. But pointing at her son only served to draw her eyes toward Marissa and her belly again. This girl would soon be a mother and be responsible for a child. But Ikee was her child and he wanted to marry some random woman just to play daddy. And her husband hadn't thought to mention any of this to her.

~~~~

"Are you really not going to say more than two words to me this entire weekend?" Kenneth asked Elizabeth as they prepared for bed.

At this point, Elizabeth was tired of holding her tongue and silently wondering about the reasons her husband would have for sabotaging her career. She wondered if the Mary Mary effect was going on in her life as well. Was Kenneth out messing around when she went on the road to promote her CDs? Was he worried that women would start coming out the woodwork once the reality show aired? My God, had she believed in this man all these years, simply to discover that he really hadn't changed at all?

He stood on one side of the bed and Elizabeth stood on the other. She kept her eyes on his, trying to detect any deception as she asked, "Are you cheating on me?"

"What?" Kenneth exploded.

"You heard me. I want you to stand there and tell me to my face that nothing is going on with you and that new secretary that you just had to hire a few months back."

"Taylor?" Kenneth's voice held an air of disbelief at the conversation he was having.

Putting her hands on her hips, Elizabeth said, "Did you hire another woman that I don't know about? Of course I'm talking about Taylor."

He didn't want to dignify Elizabeth's insult with an answer, but because she was his wife and he truly loved her, Kenneth sat down on the bed and, sounding as reasonable as a man being accused of cheating could, he said, "First off, the assistant that I have worked with for the last twenty years passed away, so I had no choice but to hire another assistant. Secondly, Taylor is Erin's age so how you could think that I'd have an affair with a woman who is the same age as my own child, I simply don't understand."

"Men do it all the time," Elizabeth said, not yielding.

"Not this man." Kenneth pointed a finger toward his chest. "The final reason your accusation is absurd," Kenneth continued through gritted teeth, "is because I love you and I wouldn't do anything to jeopardize what we have."

"I seem to remember a man who said the same kind of things to me after we'd only been married about seven years. But when all the cards were laid out, you had been cheating. And back then you even wanted to leave me for one of your skanks."

He was hot now. Lifting himself from the bed, his eyes bore into his wife. "How dare you throw that in my face as if the past twenty-five years we've been together since those early years have meant nothing." Pacing around the room, he counted off his accomplishments to her, "I gave my life to the Lord, I took care of you and my children to the best of my ability, I have been faithful to you and to the ministry the Lord put in my hands. That's it, Elizabeth, that's all I've got. And if that isn't good enough for you, then I don't know what else I can do."

Elizabeth was emotional as she listen to her husband pour his heart out to her. She loved Kenneth dearly, but sometimes she wondered if she was loving him 'right'. She knew that she was brash and sometimes overbearing, but Kenneth didn't seem to mind her personality faults. He learned to love her in spite of them. And she had spent a lot of years learning to love him in spite of those little things that irritated her. But the issue they were dealing with now wasn't as small as leaving the toilet seat up or throwing his clothes all around their bedroom.

Her career was in serious jeopardy and the man who claimed to love her wouldn't help.

"I don't understand any of this Kenneth. Because if you don't have anything to hide, why won't you agree to this reality show?"

"I have told you over and over again that I don't think we should expose the people at the homeless shelter to cameras and producers and such. What if one of the people coming to us for help has a felony and gets arrested because of your need for more fame than you already have? What if someone dies because they'd rather stay out in the cold than take the risk of being exposed at our shelter? Could you live with that? Because I can't."

"You pick the most extreme examples to trot out as the reason why you won't help me." Elizabeth plopped down on the bed, punched the pillow, and then lay down.

"I don't think you should go to sleep right now, Elizabeth. We need to talk this out." He sat down on the bed and rubbed her back, trying to get her attention. "We're leaving for our vacation tomorrow. I really don't want to go on this vacation when we're barely speaking to each other."

"Then don't go," Elizabeth told him. Then she sat up, turned to face him, and added, "Maybe I'll go without you. I need some time to think."

~~~~

"No, you did not tell Kenneth that you're going on your vacation without him!" After the conversation with Ikee and Marissa, Nina had retreated to her room and cried herself to sleep and then woke up with tears in her eyes. But now she was on the phone with Elizabeth and they were able to laugh at their trauma.

"Kenneth is working my nerves. I don't understand how he can sabotage my career and then stand in my face and claim to love me so much."

"I hear you about this sabotage stuff, because my son is over here wanting to marry some girl who is pregnant by another man."

"What is wrong with Ikee? Has he lost his mind?"

Nina was still shaking her head about the entire incident. "I don't know what's wrong with him. But I'm thinking about packing him up and getting out of this town for a little while."

"I'm glad you said that. Just because I don't want to go on vacation with Kenneth doesn't mean I want to go alone... so how about it?"

"I still can't believe you did that." Nina couldn't believe what she was hearing.

"I sure did. And I don't want a lecture on how to treat my husband right now."

Nina was thinking that she couldn't lecture Elizabeth on that at the moment, because she wasn't really speaking to Isaac either. She was just so mad about the whole thing. If Isaac had never planned that street revival, then Ikee wouldn't have knocked on Marissa's door. And none of this would be happening. Marissa probably wouldn't have given her life to the Lord either, but Nina wasn't dwelling on that. The thing she was dwelling on was that her husband had known about Marissa and never said a word to her.

"Kenneth has agreed to give me a little time away, because we both need to calm down. So, I'm calling to see if you want to go to Puerto Rico with me."

Nina screamed. "Girl, I would love to." But then she thought about what was going on at home, and quickly added, "But I can't leave Ikee."

"I wouldn't leave him either. Not with that girl sizing him up for tuxedos and wedding bands. I've got your ticket. I'm going to call the airline and change Kenneth's name to yours. While I'm doing that, I'll check to see if we can get Ikee on the flight as well."

"Wait, Elizabeth. Are you sure you want to go on this trip without Kenneth? I do need to get away. But I don't want to stop you from spending time with your husband."

"Girl, please, my husband has been talking with your husband this weekend and he has decided to stay here and help with the upcoming street revival."

"I'm so tired of hearing about those street revivals. All they're doing is bringing more and more problems into this house." Nina knew that Isaac was doing great and blessed work with those revivals, because dozens of souls were being saved with each revival. But sometimes, it seemed like the cost was just too high. Each time Isaac and Ikee left to do another revival, Nina's greatest fear was that they wouldn't return home because some thug would finally take his vengeance out on her family, once and for all.

"I know what you're saying. Kenneth is making strides with the work he does at the homeless shelter, but sometimes I think he puts his ministry before me and it's starting to get on my last nerve."

"So you really think Kenneth is okay with this?"

"After our blow out last night, that man probably doesn't want to see my face for at least a week. He'll be fine. Just check with Isaac to see if they're in need of another volunteer."

Nina was getting excited. It was time for her to stop crying and take action to save her son. "Okay, you've convinced me. Let me give you my credit card info to cover the charges."

Now Elizabeth was starting to doubt their plan. "Do you think Isaac will be okay with you and Ikee leaving with me?"

"My husband will not stand in my way. I guarantee it." If Isaac even dared to ask her and Ikee to stay here for the next street revival, she would simply remind him that her son wouldn't be considering marriage right now if it wasn't for him and this street ministry stuff. That ought to shut him up.

Chapter 9

"I don't want to go, Dad. Why is Mom suddenly coming up with this trip to Puerto Rico the day after I tell her I'm getting married?"

Isaac put a hand on his son's shoulder as they sat out on the back patio. "I understand how you feel, son. You love this girl and you want to be there for her. But a part of me wonders if you're feeling more obligation than love for this girl."

"You're wrong, Dad. Marissa is all that. She and I clicked. She gets real down on herself sometimes because she dropped out of school, but that doesn't bother me because I know that she's smart.

"Then she needs to get back into school so she'll be able to earn a living to take care of that baby."

"I know, dad. I figured that I could work at the church with you during the day and then I'd watch the baby at evening, so Marissa could attend night school."

One thing Isaac knew for certain was that the Walker men played hard, but loved even harder. At Ikee's age, Isaac thought he would be trying to stop him from running a bunch of women in and out of their house. He and Nina had dealt with that problem with Donavan and thought that it was only a matter of time before Ikee would be playing the ladies. But Ikee was a lot like his mother when it came to loyalty. Isaac had mad respect for his son because of that. But he still wasn't letting Ikee do this marriage thing without thinking it all the way through. "Coming to work with me at the church is fine. But you don't have a college degree, nor have you been to seminary, so the salary you would start at would be just above minimum wage… and that's only because I've got love for you."

"I'm not complaining, Dad. I'll start at the bottom and work my way up. Isn't that what a man is supposed to do?"

His son had come so far from the knucklehead he'd thrown out of his home after he decided to become a gang-banger that Isaac wanted to throw his arms around him and hug him. But just because Ikee wasn't thinking about street-life, didn't mean that his mind was all the way wrapped tight. "So, where will the three of you live?"

"Well," Ikee began, as if he had given the matter much thought, "since I'm not going to be making that much, and Marissa will have her hands full with the baby and night school, I think we're going to have to stay with either you and Mom or Marissa's mom. And I don't want a kid of mine growing up in the neighborhood that Marissa lives in."

"So that leaves me and your mom's house?"

"Yeah, Dad," Ikee said, as if that was the obvious solution. "I didn't think you'd want to see us on the street."

"Tell you what, son. You go on this trip with your mother and I'll talk to her about turning the basement into an apartment for you and your new family."

Ikee let out a long, suffering sigh. "You don't get it Dad. I love Marissa. Mom just wants to break us up."

Isaac stood up and leaned against the post as he said, "One thing I know for sure is if you truly love this girl, then one week away won't change that. Matter-of-fact, ten years away won't change it." Isaac knew that from experience. Because he and Nina had been apart for over a decade before they got back together. "So, start building your own family. I would count it as a personal favor to me if you did this one thing for your Mama."

With his head lowered, Ikee said, "I heard her crying last night."

"She loves you, Ikee. She only wants the best for you."

"Marissa is the best for me."

"Then, like I said, one week away won't change that."

"But the revival is in two days. Don't you still need my help?"

"Uncle Kenneth has volunteered to hang around to take up your slack on this one."

"But I'm supposed to spend the summer working with you and Uncle Keith. How can I focus on the ministry while I'm on vacation?"

"The one thing this time away will give you is a chance to talk with your mother. Help her to understand what the ministry and Marissa mean to you." Isaac's hands were tied. He wanted both his sons in the ministry with him. But his wife was hurting. He had to step back and allow God to work on his wife's heart.

He didn't want to demand that Ikee go on this trip because his son was becoming a man, and he refused to treat him like the little boy Nina wanted him to be. But Isaac was silently praying that Ikee would make the right decision.

"Okay, I'll go. But Mom will have to get used to the fact that I'm a man now, and I make my own decisions."

Isaac didn't think his wife would ever get used to that fact. But if Ikee was willing to give it the good old college try, then who was he to stand in the boy's way?

~~~~

"Pastor Isaac?" With a look of surprise on her face, Marissa said, "Ikee didn't tell me that you would be stopping by."

"I thought I should check on you since Ikee will be gone for a week." Isaac held up a grocery bag. "When my wife was pregnant she craved green grapes, ham and cheese sandwiches, Pringles, and ice cream."

A greedy smile spread across Marissa's face. "You got all of that in that bag?"

"Sure do."

She grabbed the bag. "Thank you so much, Pastor Isaac. Come on in."

Isaac sat down at the kitchen table while Marissa fixed herself a ham sandwich. He wanted to talk to her so he could see where her head was at. Ikee might think the world of this girl, but daddy needed to make sure she wasn't going to become a hindrance.

"Would you like a sandwich?" Marissa asked, after her second bite.

"No, no. I brought that stuff purely for your enjoyment."

"Thank you. And even though I have no idea why, I have been craving ham sandwiches."

"Well, you can thank my wife for that. If she hadn't been craving all those things I wouldn't have known what to bring you."

Marissa sat down at the table across from Isaac. She looked at him intently for a moment, then said, "She doesn't like me, does she?"

"Who, Nina?"

Marissa nodded, then Isaac said, "It's not that she doesn't like you. She's just concerned about Ikee. See, he was supposed to go to college but now he's decided that he's not going."

"I told Ikee not to give up on college. He's real smart and deserves a chance to go out into this world and do great things. But Ikee won't listen to me. He thinks he has to stay here and help me with the baby."

"He wants you to go to night school so you can get your GED. Ikee thinks you're smart enough for college, too. And he wants to help you get there," Isaac told her.

Shaking her head, with tears glistening in her eyes, Marissa said, "I never met nobody like Ikee before."

Sitting there, watching the emotions dance across Marissa's face, Isaac knew for certain that love existed between his son and this girl. She had his heart and he had hers. He didn't feel like questioning Marissa any further. What God joins together, let no man come between it.

He stood to leave and handed Marissa his business card after writing his cell number on the back. "If you need anything at all, don't hesitate to call me. It's my job to look after you while Ikee is gone."

Giggling, while popping a few grapes in her mouth, she said, "Okay, Pastor Isaac. I'll do that. Thank you so much for these grapes and the other stuff too."

Isaac got back in his car, heading home so he could pick up Kenneth. They had a few more items to go over before tomorrow's revival. Kenneth had checked out of the hotel and was hanging out at the house with Isaac for the week. But since Isaac left the house early this morning, he decided to let Kenneth sleep in. As he turned the corner, his cell rang. Isaac could see that it was Keith so he answered by hitting the talk button on his steering wheel. "Why you stalking me, man.

Didn't I tell you that me and Kenneth would hook up with you by noon?"

"You need to get down to the revival location right now."

Keith's voice was all business. Something was wrong. "I can get over there in about an hour. Just have to go to the house and pick up Kenneth."

"Kenneth is with me," Keith told him. "I swung by your house this morning, but you were already gone. Kenneth was up and ready to roll, so he came on out to the location with me and Cynda."

Making a U-turn, Isaac said, "I can be there in ten. But can you tell me what's going on? You don't sound so good."

"This you've got to see to believe, man. I'm just standing here tripping. Get here quick."

"I'm on my way." It was a rough side of town. The residents had suffered long and hard through poverty and despair after watching family and friends being gunned down in the streets. The blood of innocent and not-so-innocent souls called out to Isaac as he made his way to the empty lot where they had erected the tent for tomorrow night's revival.

When he'd scouted out the location with Ikee several months ago, Isaac remembered Ikee saying, "This area looks like the life has been sucked out of it," as they drove up to the empty lot.

Isaac had shaken his head in agreement. "This has been an undesirable part of town for many decades now. So much poverty and neglect allowed for the drug trade to run rampant. People like the man I used to be drove the spirit and the will to thrive out of this community. So, it's only fitting that I should help in some small way to bring it back."

"It's way past time for them to receive the kind of help the Lord can bring," Ikee had said.

"Way past time," Isaac agreed. But as he pulled up to where the tent was supposed to be, he saw Keith, Kenneth, Cynda, and a few members of the church walking around the lot, picking up pieces of the tent as they flew in the wind, and Isaac wondered if help had come too late for this community.

"What happened here?" Isaac asked as he got out of the car.

"Someone cut the tent up." Keith bent down and picked up another piece. "And that's not all." Keith pointed to the broken down wooden fence behind the lot. "They left us a message."

Cancel the revival, or die here.

"I guess they got straight to the point," Isaac said, as he read the menacing words that had been left for them.

"Why would the people in this community be against a church event that can only help them?" Kenneth wanted to know.

"We're not fighting this battle against the people. The Enemy has been against these revivals from the very beginning. He's trying to wreak havoc in my home, at the church, and even at the very location of the event. But he is not going to win this fight," Isaac assured everyone.

One of the volunteers spoke up, "But we don't have a tent anymore, Pastor. These people are not going to want to sit in this hot sun without some type of covering."

Another volunteer said, "If we can't get another tent, we're sunk."

"And you and I both know who did this," Keith said to Isaac.

Before Isaac accepted Christ into his life he would have shot a man for this kind of disrespect. Even years after putting his gun down and picking up a Bible, Isaac found himself fighting his own battle against the man who had shot Donavan and Nina. Isaac still got shivers when he thought of what he was capable of, even after saying yes to the name of Jesus...

Isaac had left the hospital after checking on Nina and Donavan. He'd wanted to pray, to ask God to fight this battle for him. But that old frenemy—anger and murder—grabbed hold of him and, before Isaac knew it, he had picked up a Glock and was on his way to find Mickey, the man responsible for the nightmare he was now living through.

Mickey was drunk when Isaac walked in on him, so drunk that slapping him upside the head with his Glock was useless. Isaac did it anyway.

The head trauma caused Mickey to vomit on the already nasty, dirty floor.

Good, Isaac thought. Some of the drunk probably oozed out of him when he threw up. Now he'll be able to feel this kick.

"Urrrgggh!" Mickey screamed as Isaac kicked him in the back.

Isaac then sent a heavy handed blow to Mickey's head.

"Ah man, that hurt!" Mickey's wobbly hand reached for his gun. Isaac ripped it out of his holster, and kicked him again.

Several kilos decorated the dilapidated dining room table. Back in the day, Isaac would have killed this low-life, taken his stuff, and sold it himself. Had he just crawled back into his past? He might as well take that stash and get his grind on. He sure wasn't going to have a church job to go back to after this, and a man's got to eat.

"I-Isaac, man, I'm sorry," Mickey said with a pained expression on his face.

Reaching down, Isaac grabbed a fist full of Mickey's shirt and pulled him up. "You messed with the wrong one, boy."

Nervously, Mickey laughed. "You know how I am, man. I just get to trippin' sometimes."

Trippin'? Was he crazy?

The answer to that stupid question was a resounding aboleet, aboleet, that's a yes, folks.

Although crazy, Mickey was no punk. He wasn't going out like a sucka, even if he was up against the great Isaac Walker. They tussled. Isaac dropped his gun. Mickey used that opportunity to swing.

With the way Isaac's jaw shook, Mickey could have been a contender. "What you think about that?" Mickey asked while shuffling his feet like a boxer. "Yeah, I ain't no easy win," He swung on Isaac again and connected.

Isaac grabbed him by the throat and drove him against the wall.

Mickey's breath whooshed from his body.

The wall buckled as Isaac slammed Mickey's head into it again and again. When he released him to grab his Glock, Mickey crumpled to the floor holding his throat. "Man, you're supposed to be a preacher."

Isaac smiled sinisterly. "That's why you're getting a two-for-one special today— a man who can kill you and preach at your miserable funeral."

Isaac kicked Mickey in the face, then picked his gun off the floor and lifted it to Mickey's head. "What do you want on your tombstone, Mickey?"

Blood dripped from his mouth, but that didn't stop him from running it. "You tired of looking at yourself, Isaac? Is that why you want me dead?"

"You're nothing like me."

Mickey crawled on the floor like the animal he was. His gold teeth weren't as sparkly with blood splattered on them. "I am what you made me. You taught me everything I know." Mickey's gun was in sight, he kept crawling toward it.

Shoot him. No need for conversation. What are you waiting on? Don't you dare think about God. Just leave the Almighty-oh-so-busy-One out of this. All these thoughts ran through Isaac's mind as Mickey reminded him of the man he used to be. "I didn't teach you to kill kids."

Mickey's laughter bounced off the walls. He picked up his gun and fired. The bullet missed Isaac by a mile. Mickey stood, more confident now. "That bad little ninja needs to die."

Mickey tried to shoot at Isaac again but his clip was empty. Isaac squeezed the trigger of his gun—he had bullets and didn't miss. The only problem was that when Mickey stood up, Isaac did not re-aim the gun and the bullet went into Mickey's left thigh.

"Urrrgggh!" Mickey dropped his gun and started jumping around while screaming, "You shot me! You shot me!"

The second bullet missed Mickey by half an inch. Slumping back to the ground, Mickey giggled through the pain. "Give me your phone, Isaac. I'm calling your pastor."

Isaac's cold eyes bore into him. "Right now, I suggest you call on Jesus."

"Forget Him. I'd rather call on the Devil. He's the only one that's ever helped me," he told Isaac, as he broke into his crazy man chant. "Oh Satan, come help me. Oh Satan, Isaac

keeps shooting at your son. Oh Satan, oh my daddy, come help me now."

Isaac's hand shook. Mickey had no idea what he was asking for, but Isaac did. The Devil would help him all right. He'd help him all the way to Hell.

"I'm bleeding. Woo hoo!" His head flopped back and forth. "I'm a bloody mess. Losing con-scious-ness." His words were slow and slurred.

He was conflicted. Should he pray or should he shoot. Finishing Mickey off would do the world a great service, but Mickey would bust Hell wide open. Even this psychopath wasn't ready for the torment he'd suffer in Hell. Isaac had already sent too many people there. Could he live with one more?

What am I doing here? How could I have sunk so low again? Isaac put his hand to his head, the one that didn't hold his Glock, and rubbed his temple. "Oh God, I don't want to send him to Hell. Help me!"

The door to the crack house opened and Keith rushed in. Isaac turned his gun on him, then lowered it. He was thankful that his friend has arrived before he'd done something he would regret fro the rest of his life.

That incident had occurred twenty years ago. Isaac was no longer conflicted. Since then, the Lord had fought too many of his battles for him to start doubting now.

He watched as Cynda started walking the perimeter of the lot, praying and calling out to God for His mercy and grace over the situation. There was no need for Isaac to ever fight his own battle again in life, not when the Lord was on his side. He was thankful that Cynda was there to remind him of just what needed to be done at times like this. He stood before the volunteers and his good friends and said, "We are in the middle of a spiritual battle right now. So, before we worry about tents, or the people who we've invited to this revival, we need to invite the Lord and His angel to come down here and partake in this event with us. If the Lord wants the work in this neighborhood to continue, then He will send provisions for us."

They all joined hands. Isaac bowed his head in reverence to his Lord and Savior, Jesus Christ. Isaac had always been the head man-in-charge, never bowing to anyone, not even his mentors, until the day he finally said yes to Jesus. That was the day he realized that there was something bigger and badder than he ever could be. God would always be able to take care of Isaac's enemies, all he had to do was turn his problem over and let the Lord work them out. "Father God, in the name of Jesus, we humbly come to You now…"

Chapter 10

The sweet fragrance of Isaac's prayers drifted up to Heaven, where two angels stood outside the most magnificent pearl-laden gates collecting the prayers of humans.

Cushions of snowy white clouds then caressed the angels' feet as they made their way past the tree of life that stood bold and beautiful in the middle of the outer court. Its leaves were a heavenly green, and its fruit was succulent and enjoyed by all. Sweet blissful music could be heard throughout the great expanse of Heaven. It was the harp, but it was better than any harp on Earth; it was the guitar, but it was better than any guitar on Earth. As the music played louder, the angels' feet left the cushiony clouds and floated the rest of the way to the Holy of Holies.

While the angels were delivering prayers to the Most Holy place, Aaron, the captain of the Host left the heavenly hosts in the outer court and made his way through the inner court on his way to the Holy Place. There were innumerable mansions in the inner court, room enough for everyone. Sadly enough, the beauty and splendor of Heaven would only be enjoyed by the few that served God. As he passed by the room of tears, he glanced in and shook his head in wonderment. It still amazed him that humans had tears so precious that God would bottle and preserve them in a room as glorious as this.

He opened the door of the Holy Place and stood in the back as he heard the voices of thunder and lightning. He then heard a multitude of praises. As the voices became thunderous, Aaron joined in with them. In this place where God sits high and is lifted up, praises are sung to Him forever. His glory lovingly fills the atmosphere and joy spreads throughout His heavenly court.

His omnipotence glistened through the emerald rainbow arched above the magnificent throne. The twenty-four elders surrounding Him were also seated on thrones and clothed in white radiant robes. They wore crowns of gold on their heads.

Seven lamps of fire were burning and a sea of crystal lay at the Master's feet. In the midst of the throne and around it were four living creatures with eyes covering their entire bodies. The first living creature was like a lion, the second a calf, the third a man, and the fourth a flying eagle. Each of the creatures had six wings. They do not rest day or night, as their massive wings enable them to soar high above the thrones. Generating cool winds throughout Heaven, they bellow continuous alms to their King crying, "Holy, holy, holy, Lord God Almighty, who was and is and is to come!"

The twenty-four elders fell down before Him and worshipped, saying, "You are worthy, O Lord, to receive glory and honor and power, for You created all things, and by Your will they exist and were created." They threw their crowns before the throne in adoration. No matter what sin and immorality went on in the Earth, none of that changed the truth... God still reigns and the world would one day understand what that simple truth meant.

Thunder and lightning sparkled from the throne of Grace once more, then Michael's glorious nine-foot form stood. His colorful wings glistened as they flapped in the air. "Yes, my

Lord," he said, as he took the scrolls from the omnipotent hand that held them.

Michael stood in front of Aaron. Michael's sword was longer and heavier than the other angels' swords. Jewels were embedded throughout the handle of this massive sword, a symbol of his many victories. The belt that held his sword sparkled with the gold of Heaven. Michael had defeated the Prince of Persia more times than he cared to remember. But the enemy was getting stronger as his time drew near. Michael eagerly awaited their next meeting. It would be their last. "Here is your assignment."

Aaron took the scrolls, then said, "My General, my Prince, we will complete the mission." He pounded his chest with his fist as he added, "God be praised forever and ever!"

~~~~

As they walked into their room at the San Juan Marriott Resort, Ikee put his bag down on the bed and then made his way over to the patio window. "This is bananas. You didn't tell me we had an ocean view room."

"If we're going to be here, why not get the ocean view room?" She and Elizabeth had called the resort before they left home and changed the room from a one bedroom suite to a two bedroom. Elizabeth had a king size bed in her room, while Nina's room had double beds so she could spend every waking moment with her son in order to find a way to talk him out of throwing away his life on a girl he barely even knew.

Ikee pulled his cell phone out of his pocket as he opened the patio door and stepped out onto the balcony. "I'm taking a picture of the ocean and sending it to Marissa. She is not going to believe this."

Nina rolled her eyes. Every other sentence was something about Marissa. "I don't want you thinking about that girl at all this week."

As he clicked pictures, Ikee said, "Mom, no disrespect, but I'm old enough to make my own decisions."

She didn't have time for Ikee's puppy love syndrome, so she stepped out of their room and decided to call Isaac as she sat down on the sofa in the living room.

He picked up on the first ring. "Hey baby, how was the flight?"

"Perfect. No turbulence at all."

"I'm glad. Is the resort as nice as you thought it would be?"

"Even better," Nina assured him. "It's bananas, as your son said. He's even standing on the balcony taking pictures of the ocean and sending them to Marissa." Nina said Marissa's name in a sing-songy voice.

Laughing, Isaac said, "He hasn't stopped talking about her, has he?"

Whispering into the phone, Nina admitted, "He's driving me crazy, Isaac. I don't know what to do. Ikee is too young to be this serious about any girl. And I certainly don't want him this serious about a pregnant girl whose child doesn't even belong to him."

"Give him some time, Nina. If it's not meant to be, then it will fizzle out."

"Yeah, but I want it to fizzle out before he goes off and marries this girl." She sighed and then asked. "What's going on with you? Is everything ready for the revival tomorrow?"

"We're getting there, just taking care of a few loose ends."

Isaac was short with her and didn't sound excited as he normally did the day before one of these events. That made

Nina think he was trying to down play it for her. And at that moment she wished she had been more supportive. She had promised to work with him in this ministry, but she just hadn't been able to shake thoughts of another disgruntled hustler from Isaac's past coming to one of those revivals and killing all of them.

Her thoughts were irrational, she knew that. But Isaac had led a dangerous life, and it seemed that everyone who had ever had beef with him kept finding their way into their lives. But he was still her husband... warts and all. Even when she didn't agree with him or like what he was doing, she had said 'I do' and still meant it. "I'm sorry that I left you to deal with everything on your own."

"Hey, don't sound so sad. I want you to enjoy your vacation. And besides, I'm not alone. Keith and Kenneth are helping me. And the things the three of us can't figure out, the Lord will just have to handle."

"Thank you for being so understanding. I really do think I need this time away."

"Just don't stay too long. I miss you already," Isaac told her.

"Me too, baby... me too," she told him, just before they hung up. Then, Nina giggled as she realized that she and her husband were acting like lovesick teenagers. She was sure Ikee was on the phone with Marissa telling her how much he wished she was here with him. But instead of absence making their hearts grow fonder, Nina was hoping that the separation would kill the romance all together.

Elizabeth stepped out of her room with a royal purple cover-all over her white swimsuit. She was rocking white pumps that had a hint of a purple trim. She put her purple and white straw hat on her head along with her Gucci sunglasses and said, "I'm ready for a swim."

"I'll say you are, looking like every bit of the star that you are. If I didn't know better I'd think cameras were getting ready to follow us down to the pool."

"Don't spoil my mood. I don't want to think about all the money Kenneth is costing me by being so stubborn."

"Are you sure that Kenneth is the one who is being stubborn?" Nina got off the sofa and headed back to her room to get her swimsuit.

"Don't you dare take that man's side. You know how important that reality show is for my career, and so does my dear husband."

"Okay, I don't want to make you mad, so just let me throw on my swimsuit and then we can head down to the pool and relax."

Chapter 11

While Marissa was trying to live vicariously through the pictures Ikee sent her of an ocean so clear she could almost see the bottom of it, and the glorious palm trees that decorated a spectacular Olympic-size pool, her doorbell rang.

The old sofa she was sitting on was low to the ground, so she had a tough time getting up. Feeling a pull in her belly, Marissa held onto her swollen stomach as she made her way to the door. But with every step she took, she was thinking about that wonderful ocean view Ikee sent her a picture of. She prayed that the two of them would someday be able to take a trip like that and just bask in the sun, without a care in the world.

Marissa didn't know much about carefree days. She might not be doing much while she waited on this baby to arrive, but her days were filled with stress because she constantly worried that the water, electricity, or gas would be shut off. Her mother worked two jobs, but still didn't have enough money to keep all the bills current. So Marissa spent her day fielding calls from bill collectors. Some days she just didn't answer the phone at all.

Opening the door earlier that day and finding Pastor Isaac on her door step holding groceries had been a welcome surprised. She and her mom had been running low on food and Marissa had prayed that someone would loan her mom some money so they could go to the store. But they hadn't needed a loan at all. God answered her prayers by sending Pastor Isaac. She was new to all this praying and receiving stuff, but she was getting the hang of it.

The person on the other side of the door banged on it just as she reached it. "Hold on, I'm coming." Marissa looked out the window, and immediately regretting doing so. She only opened the door because he had looked directly into her face as she peeked out of the window. "What are you doing here?" Marissa demanded, as Calvin Jones stormed into her living room.

"What you mean, what am I doing here?" He looked at her as if she'd lost her mind. "I'm here to check on my little niece or nephew."

"Your niece or nephew?" Marissa scoffed at that. "Didn't your brother tell you? I could be pregnant by anybody in this neighborhood. So, we won't know who my baby's father is until the DNA test."

Calvin waived that comment away. "Tony was just trippin' on account of his court case and all."

"Well he can keep tripping, because I'm not about to take my baby on no prison visits to see him when we all know that if he wasn't doing time, he wouldn't bother to come see this baby."

"Now you just talking foolish. Because we Jones men take care of our kids."

"He told me to go find my baby's daddy. Does that sound like someone who wants to take care of his kid?"

"That's why I stopped by," Calvin said, as if his brother's words hadn't been hurtful; it was just Tony being Tony. "He's been trying to call you to apologize for all that."

Putting her hands on her hips in defiance, Marissa said, "I changed my number."

"Of course you changed your number," Calvin said matter-of-factly. "I wouldn't have to stop by without calling if you hadn't."

"Look." Marissa extended a hand toward Calvin's chest, backing him up. "Thanks for checking on me. But you don't have to do that. I'm fine and my baby will be fine... I've moved on."

Calvin's lip curled as if something distasteful had found its way to his mouth. "So, that's how it is, huh? All the love you supposedly had for my brother is gone, just because he's in prison and can't come over here and check on you himself?"

"Your brother left me alone before he went to prison. You can't fault me for getting the message and then moving on with my life."

The angry scowl across Calvin's face began to dissipate. "You right. I can't fault you for what my knuckle head brother did. But you could at least do one last favor for me."

Marissa had only been fifteen when she started dating Tony. She'd thought it was cool being the girl who had the bad boy wrapped around her finger. Her mother tried to warn her, but she hadn't listened. After a month of being with Tony, he started asking her to carry this bag or hold a briefcase until he could get back to pick it up. Sometimes drugs or guns had been in the bags, other times he'd had her hold a briefcase full of money. All of it had been illegal and she no longer wanted any part of that life.

Marissa opened her door as she told Calvin, "My mother will be home from work in a few, she won't be happy to see you."

"Okay girl, I got you, I got you." He headed for the door. But just before leaving, he took the strap off his shoulder and tried to hand the bag to her. "I'll be back for it in the morning."

Marissa backed away from it. She shook her head. "I've got my baby to think about... can't be holding nothing that's going to get me locked up." Silently, she prayed and asked God to deliver her from the life she once led.

"You used to be down. Now you're acting like you're too good to help us out. How am I supposed to take that?"

The murderous look in his eyes frightened her for a moment. Then it was as if she heard the Lord telling her to speak the truth to him. She opened her mouth and said, "It's not that, Calvin. I'm a Christian now. And I don't think the Lord would be pleased if I participated in criminal stuff. You feel me?"

Calvin leaned his head back and laughed. "So, you a Christian, huh? And I guess you and that Walker boy have been doing Bible study all this time."

Her eyes got big. "How'd you know about Ikee?"

"I know a lot more than you think I know. But I'll tell you what, Ms. Christian... I'll take my dirty little bag with me and I'll leave you with a piece of advice."

Marissa was just happy that Calvin was leaving and taking his bag with him. She didn't want to do anything that would cause him to change his mind, so she stood there pretending to be interested in the so-called advice he had for her.

Calvin put a hand on the doorknob as he said, "If I was you, I'd tell lover-boy not to attend his daddy's revival tomorrow." With that, Calvin stepped out of her house and closed the door behind him.

Marissa hadn't imagined that the advice would be for Ikee. She hadn't told Ikee about Tony or his brother either, for that matter. Marissa had been so ashamed of the life she'd led once she'd gotten involved with those Jones boys that she'd been trying to block the whole experience out of her mind.

Ikee was out of town. He wouldn't be at the revival tomorrow anyway, so there was no reason to tell Ikee about Calvin or Tony or anything that Calvin had to say. She could just go on forgetting about that part of her life.

~~~~

Lying on the beach, Elizabeth questioned herself every which way she could. It was unthinkable that she had accused her husband of cheating on her. After all these years, wouldn't she have recognized the signs? Wouldn't there have been some tell in the way he acted towards her? Or had Kenneth mastered the art of cheating to the point that Elizabeth could no longer tell what was real and what was distorted in her life?

"What are you deep in thought about?" Nina asked, as she came back to her lounge chair next to the pool.

Elizabeth laid her head back against the headrest of the lounge chair and turned to her friend and asked, "Have you ever doubted Isaac? After spending so many years with him, have you ever wondered if maybe he was cheating on you?"

Nina shook her head. "He got all of that out of his system before he gave his life to the Lord. I'm thankful that my husband is one of the true believers, because he's never given me a reason to doubt him in that way since we've been married."

"That's good," Elizabeth said, with tears forming in her eyes. "Doubt is a terrible thing."

Nina reached over and hugged Elizabeth. "Oh hon, don't tell me that you think Kenneth is cheating on you. Because you know that's not true."

Elizabeth hated crying or looking vulnerable in any way. But she had loved this man for so long. She wiped the tears from her face as she said, "I wish I was as confident as you are. But the truth is, I just can't come up with another reason for his refusal to help me further my career, except that he has some secret that might be dug up."

"So, this is why you asked Kenneth to stay behind and brought me to Puerto Rico instead?"

"Hey, it's better than what I did to him the first time he cheated on me." Elizabeth tried to be funny with her comment, but she sounded more hurt than comedian like.

"He's not cheating on you, Elizabeth. Kenneth is a different man than who he was all those years ago."

"And he needs to thank God that I'm a different woman than I was back then, too," Elizabeth said, as her mind drifted back to one of the blow ups they'd had after she discovered he had been cheating on her with a white woman...

After discovering that Kenneth was cheating on her, she had thrown him out of the house, but she'd come home after a long day of job hunting to find him standing by the porch with a hand on his hip, got the nerve to have an attitude, was that light-bright-just-know-he-wishes-he-was-White-no-good-freckle-faced-adulterous husband of hers. "What do you want?"

"Where are my kids, Elizabeth?"

Her head started bobbing, lip got ta' twitching. Can't nobody do attitude like a mad Black woman, and Elizabeth intended to give him plenty of it. "Funny how you remember you have kids now. Maybe you should have told that strumpet you've been laying up with that you have kids."

"Look, Elizabeth, I don't want to fight with you. I just want my kids. You put me out, I didn't want to leave, and I sure didn't want to leave my kids—they need me."

"The kids need you!" Her hands started flailing in the air. "Why you good-for-nothing ##%@!." The wind blew, dust flew up; there was definitely a chill in the air. It did nothing to cool the fierce heat from the anger Elizabeth felt at this very moment. "What about me, huh, Kenneth? Did you ever stop to think for one second that I might have needed you, or was that irrelevant?"

He looked down at the cracks in the concrete, then over at the leaves as they fell off the big oak tree in front of their house. "Oh, so now you can't even look at me. Come on, Kenneth. What's the matter, cat got your tongue?"

He still said nothing.

"Well, maybe snow flake has your tongue. Do I have to call your woman and ask her to give you permission to speak to your wife?"

He shoved his hands deep in his pockets. "I don't want to fight with you, Elizabeth, I just want to see Erin and Danae—that's all."

"Oh, really? Well people with visitation rights pay child support. Did you know that, Mister Adultery Committing man?"

He pulled his wallet out of his back pocket, counted out two hundred dollars and handed it to her. "Is that enough?"

"What, wasn't I a good enough wife to receive a little alimony?"

He counted out another two hundred and handed it to her. "Look, I'll put your name back on our joint account; you can take whatever you want. Now can I see my children?"

She threw the money at him. "No!" she said, and walked away.

Kenneth grabbed Elizabeth's arm to turn her around to face him. She immediately balled her fist and struck out. He ducked, she slipped, and her bottom hit the concrete with full force.

"I don't want to fight with you. Will you please stop?" He bent down to help her up.

Elizabeth jerked away from him and pushed on the ground as she stood up. "Tell me why you did it. Why did you do this to us?" The tears were out now, and she hated him for it. Neighbors were peeking out their windows, then came outside, taking half-full trash bags to their trashcans. Elizabeth didn't care. She wiped at her face and her disobedient eyes and stood toe-to-toe with her husband. "Why? Tell me why."

He backed up, shoulders slumped. "The last couple of years haven't been our best."

She stepped to him again. "In other words, after I had your kids," she was so close to him, so angry, that spit smacked him in the face as she said the word 'kids', "you had no more use for me."

He wiped at the spit on his reddening face. "Look, Elizabeth, you know as well as I do that we haven't been happy for a while now."

She started strutting up and down the walkway. "I knew no such thing!" She turned to face some of her nosey neighbors that had the nerve to be standing in the street watching them. "Mind your own business! Matter-of-fact, where's your husband right now, huh? That's what your nosey butts need to be figuring out." She turned back to Kenneth. "How was I supposed to know something like that, Kenneth?" She looked him dead in the face. "Am I a mind reader or something?

Cause you sure never opened your mouth to tell me you were unhappy."

His shoulders slumped again, his knee bent, and his eyes slowly glazed over as they became cold and withdrawn. The look in his eyes sent a chill through Elizabeth.

"If you cared anything about me, you should have been able to tell how I was feeling. You should have been able to read my body language."

Oh she was good and mad now. Read it in his body language. Ha! Okay, she wasn't blind. Yeah, she could see he was unhappy. Matter-of-fact, he looked more than unhappy. Kenneth quite nicely projected the image of a poor, rejected, freckle-faced stepchild. But she was always so busy with the kids, the house, the bills, the dog, and oh my goodness, when she finally got around to his needs - that didn't take any thinking, no mind reading. What did he want from her? Forget it. She threw her hands up and walked away from him. He didn't try to grab her this time, but as she reached the top step, he called out to her again.

She spun around to face him, all the while thinking, you are a strong Black woman, you will get through this.

"I miss Erin and Danae. When can I see them?"

She struck a pose for him and said, "Read it in my body language."

After all these years, Elizabeth still hadn't figured out how to read her husband's body language. She only prayed that what he had been displaying to her was the truth, and that Kenneth still loved and adored her and wasn't willing to lose his wife over some fling. But if he wasn't having an affair, then what was the problem? Elizabeth desperately needed the Lord to give her a clue or something.

Chapter 12

"Honestly, though, I don't know what has gotten into Elizabeth. I haven't given that woman one reason to suspect that I'm cheating on her," Kenneth told Isaac and Keith, as the three of them sat around Isaac's kitchen table sharing a bucket of chicken, greens, and baked beans—compliments of Kentucky Fried Chicken.

"Seems like it's something in the water, because Nina has been tripping on me lately too." Isaac shook his head. "She's giving me more grief recently about my ministry than she ever gave me when I was rocking it in the streets."

"What's that about, though?" Keith asked, a perplexed look on his face.

"It started after Lou and Bobby-Ray tried to get even with me for what we did to their fathers by harming Ikee... Nina has been through so much already because of my past."

"No doubt," Keith interjected. "There was that other time that Mickey came after Donavan and ended up shooting both Nina and Donavan."

Then Kenneth added, "And when that crazy woman tried to kill Iona to get back at you for killing her father, Nina and Elizabeth stayed up the whole night praying in order to get y'all out of that situation."

"Okay, okay." Isaac held up a hand. "I don't need any more reminders of what my past sins have done to this family.

Y'all haven't forgotten and neither has Nina. As much as she may have tried to forgive and forget... I just don't think she's there yet. I really can't blame her though. I mean, look who she married. And on top of that I know this whole thing is eating at her because the woman lives by the rule of 'forgive and forget'. But too much has happened for Nina to be able to cast anything out of her mind. So, we're stuck right now."

"Looks like Elizabeth and I are stuck too. I always thought that she had not only forgiven me for the affairs I had early on in our marriage but, just like God does with our past sins, she had chosen to forget about it and count me as a new man. But when she accused me of cheating on her with no basis for the accusation at all, I realized that my wife/probation officer has had me on lock all these years, just waiting for me to step out of line so she could pounce."

"But did you step out of line?" Isaac asked. Isaac figured that the problems in his marriage were caused by his past dirty dealings. So, yeah, he could own the fact that he had given Nina plenty of cause for the way she was acting. But Isaac also knew that Elizabeth could be a handful at times.

"Of course not. I wouldn't dream of being unfaithful to my wife. She's just giving me grief because according to her, I must be trying to hide some secret if I don't want to do this reality show with her."

"What's your secret?" Keith asked.

"I'm an open book, man. I told her that I think this reality show is not good for us because I don't want to put the people who come to the homeless shelter on display. And, this might be a little selfish of me, but I don't want to be on display either."

"From what I've seen of those reality shows, they seem to bust up a lot of marriages," Isaac said.

"Thank you." Kenneth high-fived Isaac for the comment. "And I'm not trying to lose my marriage just so Elizabeth can sell a few more CDs. That just doesn't make sense to me."

Keith got up from the table. He opened the fridge and pulled out a soda, all the while grinning and chuckling as he came back to the table.

"What's got you so tickled?" Isaac asked.

Keith pointed from Isaac to Kenneth. "The two of you. My wife was supposed to be the bad girl of the bunch, but she's not giving me half the grief your wives are giving you."

"That's because she brought all the drama at the beginning of the marriage. She probably thinks that you'll pack your stuff and get gone if she causes you one more problem," Isaac told his friend, now laughing as well because Cynda had been a serious mess back in the day.

Isaac had dated her first, but he couldn't deal with her because she had too many issues. However, Isaac had no idea that when he and Cynda called it quits that she was pregnant. Years later he discovered that he had a daughter that Cynda never told him about. Iona came to live with him when Cynda went on trial for murdering her pimp. Once Cynda had been cleared of that murder, Keith got it in his head that God wanted him to be with Cynda. Isaac had tried to warn him that the girl was nothing but trouble. Now, Isaac was thankful that Keith hadn't listened to him, because after all these years, Cynda turned out to be all right. They had even managed to become friends.

"I'm going to tell her what you said," Keith said as he kicked his feet up on the table and leaned back in his chair like a man without a problem in the world. "But I'm real sorry that the two of you are having these problems with your women."

"Yeah, sure you are," Isaac said, knowing that Keith was thoroughly enjoying this moment. But he wasn't hating, after all that Cynda put Keith through at the beginning of their marriage, homeboy deserved all the peace he could get.

"One thing is for sure," Kenneth began, "when Elizabeth gets back here, she and I are going to have it out. I am going to make that woman understand that I'm not willing to tear down the beautiful marriage that we worked so hard for, just so she can feel like queen bee of the gospel music industry once again."

Isaac wanted to give Kenneth a big 'atta-boy', because he liked the way Kenneth was talking about standing up to Elizabeth. In Isaac's opinion, Kenneth didn't do that enough, and that was just what Elizabeth needed. But at the moment, Isaac didn't know how to solve his own problem with Nina, and until he could handle his own business, he wasn't about to get in anybody else's.

They had been sitting around Isaac's kitchen table while they waited for an email to come through letting them know if another tent was available. Isaac's iPhone beeped, letting him know a message was waiting. He picked up his phone, read the message, and then told Keith and Kenneth what it said. "Here's the deal. They have an extra tent, but all their workers are already out at other locations. So if we want it, we'll have to put it up ourselves."

"So why are you looking like we just lost hope?" Keith asked.

"Maybe we can round up some of the young men from the church," Isaac said, still looking as though he thought the task was too much for them.

"What are you saying?" Kenneth began to laugh. "You think we're too old to put that tent up?"

"You two are good friends, so I don't want to be responsible for a broken hip or your back going out."

"What he's saying is, we're too old," Keith said, then stood up and flexed his muscles. "But Isaac can speak for himself, because I still have a lot of miles left in this old tank."

"Okay then, old man, let's go get this tent." But as the three of them headed to the car, Isaac said, "I think I'll see if I can get a few of the ministers to meet us at the spot."

Both Kenneth and Keith quickly agreed, "That's a good idea. These young ministers need to experience the grunt side of ministry.

~~~~

After receiving their orders from the captain of the Host, Brogan, Nathan, and Arnoth descended from Heaven down to Earth. They had on white work shirts, boots, and overalls.

Isaac got out of his SUV and started passing out gloves to the workers. As he stood in front of Brogan , Nathan, and Arnoth, he smiled, "You boys came prepared to work. I like that."

"We believe in your ministry, Pastor. So, we just want to help in any way possible," Brogan told his charge. He'd been watching over Isaac for many years now, but this was the first conversation he'd ever had with him. He was thankful that the captain of Host still trusted him when it came to Isaac's safety.

He'd had a couple of close ones. Isaac had been shot on his watch and had been knocked unconscious, but, through it all, Brogan had kept his charge alive. He prayed that he would do a better job of protecting Isaac this go around.

They got to work building the tent. The men were in good spirits as they discussed the upcoming revival. Some had helped out at the other street revivals and they were busily giving an account of all the souls that had given their lives to the Lord. Another volunteer walked toward the back fence, pointing as he asked, "Has anyone seen this?"

He was pointing at the words 'cancel the revival or die here'.

Isaac popped the trunk on his SUV and told the volunteer, "I'm glad you mentioned that." He pulled out a can of white paint and a paint brush. "I almost forgot to cover that up."

Arnoth nudged Brogan. "Your charge has a knack for ticking people off."

"He is a much needed warrior in this fight for souls. And I'm honored to go to battle for him."

"Good, because it looks like we're going to be doing some of that sooner than we thought," Nathan said as he turned Arnoth's and Brogan's attention to the hills from which evil was lurking.

"Let's get this tent finished so we can take care of these demon spawns before they can wreak havoc on the humans." With that said, Nathan shoved the last three poles into the ground while Brogan and Arnoth pulled the covering above the poles and then secured the tent to the poles.

Keith's mouth hung open as Isaac said, "We've been out here struggling with this tent for two hours now, and the three of you put the finishing touches on it within minutes. That's got to be some kind of record for putting up a tent that will fit at least five hundred people underneath it."

"We're just doing our part." Brogan stood staring at Isaac a moment too long. This was his charge and he prayed that he would be able to deliver Isaac from the evil that wanted to take him out. But there was no time to lose. The demonic forces were steadily approaching, so they needed to get busy kicking some demon butt. "All the best to you, Pastor. We will see you tomorrow."

"Where are you going?" Isaac asked. "Don't you remember? I'm treating all the volunteers to pizza."

"We can't stay, but thanks for the offer." Brogan put a hand on Isaac's shoulder, squeezed it and then released as he and his crew walked away from them.

"You weren't supposed to touch him. You are tempting fate and Captain Aaron will not like that one bit," Nathan said self-righteously.

"Oh, you mean the same way you tempted fate when you pulled Kenneth out of the rubble that had once been the World Trade Center?"

Nathan couldn't answer for himself, but Arnoth had no trouble jumping in. "That was a life or death situation. Kenneth would have died if Nathan hadn't pulled him out when he did. But you are testing fate at your whim. We weren't supposed to even talk to these humans, but since you're in charge we had to follow your lead. And now look at what you've brought down on us." Arnoth pointed to the cloud of dust that was barreling toward them like a whirlwind.

"Save it Arnoth, because you didn't have a problem with talking to your charge. If I recall correctly, you were even knighted for the way you handled Cynda." Brogan had no more time for talking, his workman clothes disappeared as he pulled out his sword. "Let's take care of business."

Nathan and Arnoth pulled their swords out and joined Brogan as they stood in the middle of the street. Brogan lifted his sword and shouted, "By the God I serve and His son Jesus Christ, I command you to halt!"

The whirlwind stopped, but that's when the trouble began. They were now face to face with the biggest, ugliest, grizzly-looking demons they'd encountered in years. Their heads were like bats and they had ten-inch fangs. Nathan had dealt with demons like these when he'd pulled Kenneth out of that rubble. It was the worse fight he'd ever been in. He turned to Brogan and said, "This won't be easy."

"It never is," Brogan told him as he charged into the fray, screaming, "It ends here! You will not defeat the man of God!"

"We've already defeated him. You just don't know it yet," one of the demons spat the words out. They were his last, because within the next second, Brogan had split him in two.

They went on and on throughout the night. The rain descended and they kept fighting. The electricity went out in homes all around town. The homeowners call the electric companies and trucks were sent out to repair the lines, but after one line was repaired another would be knocked down, until the workers finally gave up. They decided they'd come back once the rain let up. But it didn't let up all night long.

By morning Brogan, Arnoth, and Nathan lifted their bloody swords toward Heaven and said, "For all that is holy and for all that is right."

Chapter 13

As Nina opened her eyes and stared at the sleeping form of her baby boy as he lay in the double bed next to hers, she was struck by how much he looked like his daddy—how much he looked like a grown man, a grown man who was capable of making his own decisions. Nina's eyes closed as she tried to block out the facts that were right in front of her.

Turning away from Ikee, she glanced out of the window. The ocean that seemed to go on forever was romantic and inviting, and at that moment, she was struck by one singular thing—she wanted to be with her husband. Not wanting to wake Ikee up, Nina climb out of her bed, grabbed her cell phone, and went out on the balcony.

She should have been at home with her husband, helping him with his ministry, not on vacation, basking in the sun and lying around the pool in Puerto Rico. Guilt was consuming Nina's heart, and all she wanted to do was hear Isaac's voice. It was seven in the morning. She knew that her husband preferred to sleep until eight, but this was the morning of the street revival; he had most likely gotten up an hour ago to spend some time in prayer.

The phone only rang about one and a half times before Isaac's deep, sexy voice bellowed a greeting into her ear. A tear drifted down Nina's face as she confessed, "I miss you so much."

"I was just thinking the same thing. Then I prayed and asked the Lord to send you back to me."

Nina closed her eyes and drew in a long, deep breath. "What am I doing, Isaac? Why on earth did I even considering leaving you alone at a time like this? I'm supposed to be helping you, not on vacation."

"You did what you thought was right, baby. I can't be mad at that."

There had been a time in their lives when Isaac wasn't good to her or for her. Before Isaac gave his life to the Lord, he'd never been concerned about what made her happy, not really. Isaac wanted what Isaac wanted, and what Nina wanted had always been an afterthought. But these days, her husband concerned himself with making her happy. So, if Isaac wouldn't put an end to those street revivals, Nina should have realized that they were bigger than what was between them. This was a God thing—that's why Isaac couldn't stop. "You should be mad. I left you and Keith to do God's work, while I just ran away."

"It's alright, Nina. God's got us. I have a feeling about today's event. It's going to be the best one yet."

"I'll be praying for you." Nina truly meant that. Even through her fears, she could see that Isaac was doing good work. So, she would be praying for his event and for God to give her the strength to stop standing in the way.

"How is Ikee doing?"

"Still hopelessly in love." Nina shook her head in disbelief. "I don't know if this girl is some voodoo specialist or what, but she has got our son in her pocket."

"I took her some groceries yesterday. She seemed to appreciate the effort."

Nina smiled at how kind her husband had become. "I don't know how you did it, Isaac Walker, but you have officially become the best man in the world." If Ikee didn't change his mind about marrying this girl, Nina would have to eat a lot of humble pie just to keep her family intact.

"Maybe you should take her to lunch or something," Isaac suggested.

"I think I'll keep trying to work my magic on this end. But if your son doesn't budge, I'll be making those reservations."

~~~~

"Thank you, Lord. I knew You would bring Nina around," Isaac said as he hung up the phone. He then showered and got dressed— a button-down shirt, no tie, slacks, and a sports jacket. He didn't like to over dress when he did these events. People were more comfortable with him and tended to relax and soak in the Word of God better when he appeared more approachable.

Kenneth was waiting for him in the kitchen. He had on a polo shirt and a pair of jeans. Isaac figured that Keith would most likely be wearing a polo shirt and some jeans as well. This was about winning souls, nothing else.

"You ready to go?" Isaac asked.

"Yeah, I just fixed myself coffee and a bagel with that veggie cream cheese you had in the fridge. I hope that was okay."

"Of course. That's what it's there for."

"Are you going to fix some breakfast before we leave?"

Isaac shook his head. "I can never eat before a revival. And anyway, I want to stop by Ikee's girlfriend's house to see if she wants to attend the revival with us." Isaac grabbed his keys and they left the house.

As they drove down the street, Kenneth said, "I wonder what Elizabeth is doing right now."

"I don't know what your wife is doing, but my wife called this morning and said that she missed me."

"I'm jealous," Kenneth confessed. "Elizabeth has only called me once and that was only to tell me that she had arrived safely. I guess she's still ticked off."

As Isaac pulled up in front of Marissa's house and turned the engine off, he said, "Elizabeth will come around. Her marriage is more important than some reality show." Isaac opened the door.

"Ikee doesn't even know what he's getting himself into," Kenneth said.

"He hasn't a clue," Isaac agreed. "But if they're going to do this at such an early age, I'm going to give them the best chance at success."

~~~~~

Ikee, Nina, and Elizabeth sat around the restaurant table looking lost and lonely, even though they were in a room full of people.

"Look at us," Elizabeth said, after the waitress placed their food in front of them. "We should be having the time of our lives. We're in a beautiful place with good company and good food. But you and Ikee look like you'd rather be anywhere but here."

"You don't look any better," Nina told Elizabeth. "You're pretending like you're having the time of your life, but I know you, girl. Your eyes don't pretend."

"Okay, so we're all miserable. What do we do about it?" Elizabeth asked as she picked up a piece of toast from her plate, then put it back down.

Ikee leaned forward as he said, "I don't know about y'all, but I'm ready to hitch a ride out of here."

"Even if we went to the airport right now, we wouldn't get home until tonight. So, we'd still miss the revival."

"We could get a non-stop flight. That way, I could get

home for the tail end of the revival. I'd be able to help dad with the altar call."

The look of excitement in Ikee's eyes stunned Nina. She and Isaac had prayed that all of their children would grow to be ministry minded, but now that they were, she was the one standing in their way. She wanted desperately to get out of Ikee's way, but she just didn't know how. Nina looked toward Elizabeth as she told Ikee, "I can't leave Elizabeth here all by herself."

Smiling, for the first time that morning, Elizabeth said, "Who says I wouldn't hop on that plane with you?"

"You really don't mind if we leave, Aunt Elizabeth?"

"No, Ikee. To tell you the truth, I miss my husband. I need to get back and talk to that man."

Lifting a hand, Nina suggested, "Why don't we finish our breakfast. Then we can contact the airport to find out if we can even get a flight out of here today."

Ikee jumped out of his seat, put his arms around Nina, and kissed her forehead and then both her cheeks.

"Calm down, boy, we don't even know if we'll be able to get out of here." Nina knew that Ikee was excited because he would be back home with Marissa before the night was over. She remembered being young and in love, and, for a moment, Nina regretted all thoughts of breaking the couple up. They would go home and whatever was to be, would be.

~~~~~

Marissa was so excited when Pastor Isaac invited her to the revival that she rushed to get dressed. She would have ran to the car if she wasn't carrying baby weight, because all she had been doing was sitting in the house, staring at the paint on the walls.

"I am so glad you thought about me, Pastor Isaac. I wasn't

doing a thing but sitting around watching re-runs of Law and Order."

Kenneth had gotten into the back of the car so that Marissa would have more legroom. As Isaac pulled up to a red light, he looked over at her, praying that the Lord would allow him to see into Marissa's heart, mind, and soul. He didn't know for sure if she was the right girl for Ikee, but he had a feeling that she was in their lives for a reason. "You know... Nina and I could always help out with some babysitting if you want to go back to school."

"I've been thinking about it," she admitted. "I just don't want to be a burden to anyone. And I really don't want to give Mrs. Nina another reason to dislike me."

"Nina doesn't dislike you," Isaac said quickly.

Marissa didn't believe it. In fact, she understood why Ikee's mother would be down on her. If her son brought home some random woman, saying he was in love and wanted to get married... oh and by the way, the woman I'm marrying is pregnant by another man. Yeah, Marissa would have a problem with that.

But because of Ikee, Marissa had changed. She wasn't the same person who dated drug dealers and held their illegal drugs and guns. The power of God had changed her and she wanted Ikee's parents to know that. "It's okay, Pastor Isaac. Because if Mrs. Nina gets to know me, she'll come to see that I'm not such a bad person."

Isaac smiled and patted Marissa on the shoulder as they pulled up to the location. "I'm looking forward to Nina getting to know you."

Marissa smiled back at him with joy filling her eyes. "Me too."

They got out of the SUV. Isaac and Kenneth walked

toward the stage while Marissa decided to help the volunteers put the chairs out. If she could have done more, she would have, because Ikee had told her on numerous occasions how good it made him feel to be a part of something bigger than himself.

As she sat down in one of the chairs she helped put out, Marissa imagined herself helping out in all sorts of ministry related events. There was something in this world that she was good at, and she planned to figure out just what it was. She began to pray, "Thank you for allowing me to be here today. Let me soak in the message and help out where I can. I want to be used by you."

"Is this seat taken?"

Marissa heard the voice, but she hoped it wasn't who she thought it was. She looked up and saw Dana Milner, Calvin's on and off girlfriend, = standing there. Marissa didn't know if she would have to go into a witness protection program to get away from these people. Ikee had told her that his dad's past kept coming back to haunt him; maybe she would just have to deal with the reality of her past and learn to live for the future. "Hey, Dana. I didn't expect to see you here today."

"Calvin asked me to come."

As Dana sat down next to her, Marissa noticed that she was carrying the same bag Calvin tried to get her to hold the night before. Were they planning to shoot the people attending this revival? *Lord, help me. I don't know what to do.*

Chapter 14

Nina came back from the airport counter with two tickets in her hand. "I've got good news and bad news," she told Ikee.

"You've got tickets in your hand so it looks like we're getting out of here, so I'm good." Ikee was grinning from ear-to-ear.

"Yes, but they didn't have any direct flights so we have a connector in Atlanta, which means you will not get home in time for any part of the revival."

"That ought to make you happy."

Nina sat down next to her son and handed him his ticket. "I'm not happy about this, Ikee." She shook her head. "Far from it, because for the first time in my life, I have allowed fear to dictate my actions, rather than praying and trusting God to keep you safe."

Ikee didn't understand. He turned toward his mother. "What are you so afraid of?"

Sighing as she ran a finger over her eyebrow, Nina prayed for the right words as she opened her mouth to explain. "What can I say? Your father has always been like a whirlwind in my life. Always bigger, and greater, and so much more than I ever expected to be dealing with. But I can handle all of that, because that's who he is." She hesitated, trying to focus and understand her dilemma herself. "I just didn't know that he had so many enemies, and that marrying him meant putting my kids at risk."

Ikee's eyes widened. "You regret marrying daddy?"

She shook her head. "Never. I love your father. But I have grown weary of all the collateral damage." Then, she smiled at herself for not understanding this early on as she said, "But that's also a part of who he is. He doesn't know how to back down or run and hide. So, you and your daddy don't have the problem. I do. And I'm asking the Lord to help me with that. Okay?"

Ikee put an arm around his mother's shoulder. "Okay."

That's when Elizabeth came bouncing over to them, holding up her ticket while singing, "On my way to see my man, on my way to see my man, happy, happy... oh what a happy day!"

The three of them hugged. They had left town for a vacation that was supposed to make them feel better about their situations, but the funny thing was, they hadn't started feeling better until they decided to go back and deal with their issues.

~~~~~

Isaac stood behind the podium, looking out at all the people who'd gathered under this tent to celebrate the Lord. Enemies had tried to destroy the tent and had even left a threatening message for them, but none of it mattered as Isaac got ready to preach the Word of God. He wanted to give the people something they could hold on to, because the Bible told him that many hearts would give out due to fear in these last and evil days.

He was witnessing some of that fear in his own house, with his wife. In some way, Isaac felt that if he could teach the people how to stand in times like these, then maybe he would also be able to ease Nina's fears as well. He opened his Bible and began reading from Psalms 27:

The Lord is my light and my salvation; whom shall I fear?

The Lord is the strength of my life; of whom shall I be afraid? When the wicked even mine enemies and my foes, came upon me to eat up my flesh, they stumbled and fell.

Though a host should encamp against me, my heart shall not fear: though war should rise against me, in this will I be confident. One thing have I desired of the Lord, that will I seek after; that I may dwell in the house of the Lord all the days of my life, to behold the beauty of the Lord, and to enquire in His temple.

For in the time of trouble he shall hide me in his pavilion: in the secret of his tabernacle shall he hide me; he shall set me upon a rock. And now shall mine head be lifted up above mine enemies round about me: therefore will I offer in his tabernacle sacrifices of joy; I will sing, yea, I will sing praises unto the Lord.

He closed the Bible and began speaking to the people from his heart. "In these last and evil days we can't allow man to make us afraid and cause us to give up and run away from the work God has put before us. Our mission on earth is clear... it is to do the will of God, not the will of man. So, stand up and whatever you do, never be ashamed to name the name of Jesus Christ.

~~~~

"Why hasn't the captain of host called us back yet?" Arnoth asked, a look of confusion on his face.

Brogan turned to Nathan and Arnoth and asked, "We missed something?"

Nathan shook his head. "We dispatched those demons last night and I haven't seen any more lurking around here this morning."

Pointing at the numerous people in attendance, Arnoth

clarified, "Except for the ones some of the humans brought with them."

"Yeah, but as long as those demons remain dormant inside the humans, we aren't at liberty to do anything about them. Hopefully, Isaac will cast a few of those demons out during the altar call… and then they will be all ours."

Nathan and Arnoth smiled at that.

But then Brogan said, "Remember, we are on Earth. These humans have free will. So not everything is ruled by God or the Wicked One. We foiled the Wicked One's plan last night, but mark my words, we're not done yet." It was times like these that Brogan wished that angels could see into the future just as God could, that way he would know what he didn't know and be better able to help his charge. But Satan had been kicked out of heaven for desiring to be like God, so Brogan repented of his thought and simply watched and waited.

~~~~

Marissa was soaking in every word. She had been afraid too many times throughout her life. Most of her fears came from living in an area that was infested with crime. But what Pastor Isaac was saying made sense. She could put her trust in God and let go of fear altogether, maybe then she could do the will of God like her husband and son were ready, willing and able to do.

Pastor Isaac sat down as three praise singers stepped forward and began singing. Dana chose that moment to get up; she seemed to be in a hurry, but Marissa noticed that she left Calvin's bag behind. She wasn't about to pick that bag up. What if a cop saw her with the bag and then asked to search it. She didn't know how many years she'd get for the possession of illegal guns, and she didn't want to find out.

Marissa got out of her seat and ran after Dana, but Dana

was track-staring it down the street like she wanted to be anywhere but the revival. Being seven months pregnant, there was no way that Marissa was going to catch up to Dana. She stood and watched Dana for a moment longer. That's when she noticed Calvin's black Lexus with gold rims pull up next to Dana. She jumped in the car and it sped off.

If that was Calvin, Marissa wondered why he didn't send Dana back for that bag and why he sped off like somebody was trying to carjack him. That was when she remembered that Calvin had warned her that Ikee shouldn't attend this revival, as if something bad would happen. Now, she was very curious about that bag. What had Dana left behind? She knew that it wasn't drugs or guns—no way would Dana have left Calvin's stash.

Everything in her was telling her to run… get out while the getting was good. But Marissa hadn't called Ikee yesterday to tell him what Calvin had said to her and now she was feeling guilty. If something happened to these people and she did nothing to help, Marissa wouldn't be able to live with herself.

~~~~

Everything seemed to happen in slow motion. Isaac was seated behind the podium as the praise singers encouraged the crowd to stand on their feet and worship the Lord. But as everybody stood, he saw Marissa rushing back to her seat. She bent down and opened a bag and then she started screaming. Isaac got up, preparing to see what had happened, but Kenneth put a hand on his shoulder.

"You need to be up here. The people will expect you to preach again when the praisers finish. I'll go check on her."

Isaac nodded, but by that time, Marissa was running away from the revival, still screaming while carrying the bag she'd just looked into.

Marissa reached the street before Kenneth caught up with her. She threw the bag up in the air and then tried to run back towards the revival, but Kenneth was behind her and she ran directly into him.. They both fell down and then there was a loud BOOM!

~~~~

As the pregnant girl threw the bag in the air, Brogan heard Isaac yell, "Marissa!" and then saw him step down from the podium and head toward her. "It's happening," Brogan said as he beat a path toward the pregnant girl. The bag exploded before he reached her. Marissa and Kenneth fell to the ground just as the explosives rained down on them. The force of the explosion knocked Isaac and several others in the crowd backwards as well.

Brogan threw himself toward the bag where the explosion had come from, and felt the impact as it exploded again. The second explosion was worse than the first, but as Brogan lay on it, the bomb put a hole in the ground beneath him.

Arnoth pulled Marissa off of Kenneth, her body seemed lifeless as he blew the breath of life back into her.

Nathan's eyes widened as he saw Kenneth lying there, motionless. Images of 9/11 and pulling Kenneth out of that rubble flashed before his eyes. He hadn't saved Kenneth's life all those years ago just to watch him die a senseless death.

Nathan put a hand on Kenneth, trying to give him the strength to survive this attack.

Brogan was weak from lying on that bomb, but he scanned the crowd and saw Isaac getting up and brushing his clothes off. His charge was okay. He hadn't lost him this time. *Good*, Brogan thought as he started to drift off.

Chapter 15

"Nina, where are you?!" Isaac screamed into the phone. "Ikee and Elizabeth aren't answering their phones either and I need to speak with both of them."

Isaac, Keith, and Cynda were at the hospital, praying for the numerous people who'd been brought into the emergency room with cuts, bruises, and broken bones. Keith and Cynda weren't at the Revival when the bomb went off because they were driving the church van, picking up neighborhood kids and bringing them to the event.

Isaac was thanking the good Lord that Keith and Cynda had not returned to the revival with those kids. If one of those children had been harmed, he didn't know if he would've been able to forgive himself. He was having a hard enough time coming up with a reason to forgive himself for not canceling the revival after repeatedly being warned to do so.

Kenneth was unconscious and Marissa was in surgery. At this point, the doctors weren't sure if they would be able to save both mother and child. So he stood there and listened while Marissa's heartbroken mother instructed the doctors to do everything to save her daughter's life. The woman then sat down in the waiting room and cried like she was proactively mourning the death of her grandchild.

Isaac had tried to get a hold of Ikee and Nina before Marissa went into surgery, but neither had answered their phones and now he was worried that something might have happened to them. And knowing that Nina and Ikee would have been at home with him if he had just canceled the revival like Nina had practically begged him to do, Isaac felt like sitting in the chair next to Marissa's mother and crying his sorrows out too. But he couldn't break down now, not when so many people needed him to be strong.

Isaac got back on his cell phone and call Johnny. He hadn't been at the revival today because he was working a case. When Johnny picked up, Isaac told him that he thought Calvin Jones was responsible for the explosion. "He threatened me, but I didn't listen."

"That name just keeps coming up today," Johnny said. "Let me do some checking, and I'll get back with you."

As Isaac hung up the phone, the emergency room was being flooded with wounded people once again. But this group hadn't been at the revival—they were all busted up after participating in a riot. Calvin Jones strikes again. Isaac was weary from all the destruction. He went for a walk around the hospital; he needed to find a spot so he could be alone and talk to God about this, because Isaac just didn't understand.

~~~~

"That flight was terrible," Nina said, as she, Elizabeth, and Ikee rushed to get to their connecting flight. The Atlanta airport was a gigantic. They had to ride a shuttle and take several flights of stairs in order to get to the terminal for their next flight.

"I'm just glad to be on the ground. I'm thinking about renting a car and driving to Dayton rather than getting on this next plane."

"That's an eight hour drive, Aunt Elizabeth. I'm not trying to do that. I need to get home to my girl."

Nina rolled her eyes. "Boy, can your mind function to think about anything but Marissa?"

"Nope. Matter-of-fact, I need to call her. Let me use your phone."

Nina shook her head. "I've got you to myself for at least another few hours. You can talk to me about your plans for your future. You can talk to Marissa when you get home."

Ikee turned to Elizabeth. "Let me borrow your cell, Auntie."

"Don't put me in the middle of this. You better charge your own cell phone or sit down and talk to your mother."

They arrived at the terminal. Elizabeth pulled out her cell and turned it back on as she said, "But I do need to call my man and let him know that I'm on my way back."

"Nooo!" Nina grabbed the cell from Elizabeth. "I told you I wanted to surprise Isaac. If you call Kenneth, he's going to know that I'm on my way home too."

"They're probably still at the revival anyway. That's why y'all need to let me use the phone so I can call my girl," Ikee told them.

Nina started to hand Elizabeth her phone, but as it buzzed to life she noticed several calls from Isaac scrolling down the screen. "Why is Isaac blowing up your phone?"

"I don't know." Elizabeth took the phone from Nina. "Let me see if he left a message."

Nina took her cell out of her purse and turned it on.

"He didn't leave a message," Elizabeth said, after checking her voicemail messages.

Nina's phone powered on. She had several calls from Isaac as well, and he had left her numerous messages. She listened to the last message and then got out of her seat. "I'll be right back," she told them. "Sounds like something's up."

It was a little loud in the terminal area, so Nina walked over to the narrow hallway by the bathroom and made her call.

When Isaac picked up the phone she could hear the stress in his voice. "Baby, what's wrong? You don't sound right."

"Nina." There was sorrow in his voice as he said, "I need you home now."

She would have tried to be coy and not informed him that she was about to get on her connector except something in his voice told her that he didn't need games right now. "We left Puerto Rico this morning. We should be home in a few hours."

"Thank God." He sounded relieved.

"What's going on, Isaac?"

"I need you to talk to Elizabeth and Ikee for me…"

~~~~~

The flight attendant said, "Welcome to Dayton. Give us just a few more minutes and then we will open the door."

"No!" Elizabeth screamed. "I can't stay in this seat one second longer." The flight from Puerto Rico to Atlanta had been turbulent, but after Nina told her that Kenneth was unconscious and lying in a hospital bed, all she could think about was the fact that her selfishness had put him there. If she hadn't left him in Dayton after deciding to take her vacation without him, she and Kenneth would be on the beach right now.

"Yeah, let us off this plane," Ikee shouted out to the flight attendant.

"The hatch is coming down now, just be patient," the flight attendant told them.

But Elizabeth started crying. Her tears didn't let up until they let her off the plane after landing and she was at the hospital, sitting in front of Kenneth's bed.

"I'm so sorry, baby. I'm so sorry," she kept telling him, hoping that he would hear her, wake up, and tell her that he had already forgiven her. The only problem was that Elizabeth didn't know if she would ever forgive herself.

She had been selfish, only thinking of herself and her career. She needed Kenneth to wake up so she could listen, *really* listen, to everything he had to say. "Come on, baby, wake up and talk to me."

~~~~~

Isaac hugged Nina and Ikee. He then took Ikee to the side and said, "Marissa is out of surgery. But I need to tell you something before you go in to see her."

"Why did she have surgery, Dad? I don't understand."

"I don't know if the fall did it or the explosion, but she had some internal bleeding and the doctors had to do a c-section to get the baby out immediately." Isaac lowered his head for a moment, then he looked his son square in the eye. "The baby didn't make it."

"What?!" Ikee couldn't believe what he was hearing. "I—I have to see her."

"Go on in, Son. Just be strong for her, okay?"

Ikee didn't know if he could be strong as he saw Marissa lying in the hospital bed, holding her stomach. He sat down next to her bed and laid his head on her shoulder.

Marissa ran her hand across his head as she told him, "I was praying that you would come to see me."

"I'm here, Marissa. I'll always be here for you."

She tried to smile but it got lost on her tear drenched face. "Can you stay here with me tonight."

"I'll ask the nurse to bring in a cot. I won't leave you. I promise."

~~~~~

Johnny called back and Isaac quickly answered the call.

140

"Sorry I had to hang up like that, but we were in the middle of settling down that riot on the east side of town."

"So Calvin planned a riot on the east side of town and an explosion on the west side... for what? I just don't get it." Isaac didn't understand why Calvin would cause such destruction. There had to be a reason.

Johnny said, "We just picked Calvin up. He was in the middle of the biggest drug buy of his criminal career. Too bad it was with an undercover cop."

"So, you all knew what he was up to all along?"

"No, not at all. We would have never stood by and just let him set off a bomb in this city." Johnny told him, "We knew about the riot, and we had police dispatched for that. But all of it was smoke and mirrors. Calvin wanted the police force so inundated with one crisis after another, so he could flood the city with tons and tons more drugs."

"I must be getting old, Son-in-law, because when Calvin first approached me, I never even considered that what his true purpose was." But it all made sense to Isaac now. Calvin never really wanted them to cancel that revival. He had been fishing for information the whole time and Isaac had played right into his hands.

"You're only as old as you feel. And with the way you get around, I don't see you and Nina in a retirement home any time soon."

"Thanks for calling back. Hopefully, you'll be able to connect Calvin to the explosion. He caused too much destruction today, and he should answer for it." Calvin's need for a diversion had caused the death of a child... one that would have been his grandchild once Ikee and Marissa married. So, Isaac was feeling some type of way about that. He wanted justice for that baby. But instead of picking up a gun and going after Calvin himself, Isaac went home and prayed about it.

Chapter 16

Huddled in a corner, Elizabeth knees were pulled up to her chest as she cried and prayed and cried some more. Her husband hadn't woke up yet. The doctors were giving her that look, causing her to believe that they didn't know what to do either.

The last time Kenneth had been knocked unconscious and then brought to the hospital was during 9/11. By the time he opened his eyes, Kenneth had no clue who he was nor did he remember his family. Elizabeth had spent years looking for her husband to no avail. When he finally had returned home, they spent another year re-introducing him to his family and friends.

She couldn't go through that again. She prayed, "Lord, please let Kenneth be okay. And let him remember me."

"Of course I remember you," a groggy voice said.

Elizabeth pulled herself off the floor and rushed over to Kenneth's bed. "Baby, did you say something?"

"Head hurts," was his only response.

Elizabeth hit the nurse button. "I'll get someone in here to check on you. But Kenneth, can I ask you something?"

He nodded.

Holding her breath for a second, she exhaled and then asked, "What's my name?"

"Stop worrying, I don't have amnesia, Elizabeth. You are my wife and I am thankful that God brought us together."

Elizabeth wrapped her arms around her husband. "I'm so glad that you came back to me. I don't know what I would have done… if — if." She couldn't get the words out.

Kenneth put a hand to her lips. "I'm not going no where. So just calm down, okay."

The nurse came into the room and checked on Kenneth. Once she left, Elizabeth spent the rest of the night by his side, talking to him when he was awake or just watching him sleep. She didn't mention on word about the reality show, which was no longer important to her. Kenneth was alive. She was number one with him and that was good enough.

~~~~

Marissa lay on her left side, watching Ikee sleep. He was so handsome that she could spend a lifetime watching him and never regret one second of the time spent. But she worried that Ikee would eventually have regrets if she didn't give him the chance to be all he could be.

Touching her stomach, Marissa reminded herself once again that the baby was gone. She would grieve the death of her baby for years to come, but Marissa made up her mind right then and there that she would move forward. She had spent the weekend soaking in everything Pastor Isaac said and because of his words, she was no longer afraid to dream.

Ikee opened his eyes and saw her staring. He asked, "How long have you been awake?"

"For a little while."

"Why didn't you wake me? I'm here to keep you company. Not to be sleeping while you're up."

"It was fine," she told him. "I've been thinking about a lot of things this morning. I was just waiting on you to wake up so I could tell you about my thoughts."

Wiping around the edges of his eyes, Ikee sat up. "I'm all ears. We can talk about whatever you want."

"How about college?" she said quickly.

"What about it?"

"You got accepted into a couple of colleges, but you just blew them off once we decided we were going to be together."

He shrugged. "So."

"Don't you see, Ikee. I'm not having a baby anymore." She paused for a second as if she had to let those words sink into her heart. "You don't have to marry me right now."

He got off the bed and came closer to her. Putting his hands on the bed rail he said, "I thought you wanted to marry me?"

"I did… I do… But not now. We're both too young and you need to go to college."

"No," he told her, "I'm not leaving you."

"Yes, you are." Tears drifted down Marissa's face. It was hard giving him up, but she knew it was the right thing to do. That saying, 'if you love someone, set them free. If they comes back to you, they're yours, was was rambling through her head as she said, "And when you come back, I'm going to finally have something interesting to talk to you about because I'm going to get my GED, and then I'm going to go to college too."

"But what about us? We can get married and have a— another baby." He stumbled over his words, but he wanted her to know that he was still into raising a family with her.

"Let's do all of that. Promise me you'll come back for me after you graduate."

"I don't have to promise, because I'm not leaving."

"I won't marry you unless you leave. You're smart Ikee. You deserve the chance to see what you can become in this world."

"We can become something together."

"I'm getting tired, Ikee. I need to go back to sleep. But before I do, promise me that we'll meet up... have dinner or something after we both graduate from college."

He didn't respond at first.

"Promise me," Marissa repeated as tears clouded her eyes even as they closing so she could sleep.

He wiped the tears from her face and gave his word, "I promise."

~~~~

As Nina and Isaac lay in bed that morning, Isaac said, "I should have listened to you. So many people were harmed because I refused to cancel that revival."

Nina put her finger to Isaac's lips. "Don't talk like that. You are doing the will of God and ain't no shame or blame in that."

"I messed up, baby. I played right into Calvin's hands. I've been out of the game so long that I didn't even recognize the trap that was being laid out for us."

"Don't be so hard on yourself, Isaac. You're not the only one who fell for a trap. I was so afraid that Ikee would get hurt if he helped out in the family business that I tried to escape with him. And he ended up getting hurt anyway. It broke my heart to leave him at that hospital last night. Did you see the look in his eyes?"

"Marissa is his first love. He's going to be in pain for a long time behind this. But he'll eventually get over it."

"Will he, Isaac? Will he forgive me? Because if I had let him stay here, Marissa might not have gotten hurt in the first place."

Wrapping his arms around his wife, Isaac told her, "Don't beat yourself up over this. You did what you thought was best. Ikee won't hold that against you."

"I was just wrong on so many levels. I let fear guide me instead of listening to the voice of God, which would have clearly told me to stay right here with you. Come what may, we must do the will of God."

"Even if it means getting hurt in the process?"

Nina nodded. "I may not like it, but even if something happens to one of us, we must still follow Christ."

"So does that mean you'll be with me at the next revival?" He could hardly believe he was asking, especially after he'd barely escaped being blown to bits, but he had to know where Nina's head was at.

It only took Nina a moment to answer. "I will be with you."

He leaned forward and kissed her, thinking about how good God was. He was able to take care of everything that concerned Isaac, even his wife. "I love you, baby."

"I love you more, Isaac Walker. And you can't do a thing about it."

Epilogue

After two days in the hospital, the doctor cleared Kenneth to fly. Elizabeth took her husband home and never uttered another word to Kenneth about the reality show. She came to understand his concern with how a show like that could affect their relationship. Her new CD was number twelve on the Gospel Music charts. But even if Elizabeth never had another number one hit, she was content with the love that she and Kenneth had.

Nina was front and center at Isaac's next revival. She no longer let fear grip her heart because she much preferred to be in the will of God.

Ikee and Marissa both went off to college. They made plans to have dinner after they graduated. Marissa made the reservations and stayed at the restaurant for two hours waiting on Ikee, but he never showed. Marissa was heartbroken because she had so much to tell Ikee. She prayed that one day she would get the chance to share everything that was in her heart.

The end…

But it's not the end of Ikee and Marissa's story. If you want to know if these two ever get together, then stay tuned for the final book in the Rain series…

(**Sunshine and Rain**) rel. date January, 2016

Coming in January 2016… Sunshine and Rain

Don't forget to join my mailing list:
http://vanessamiller.com/events/join-mailing-list/
Join me on Facebook: https://www.facebook.com/groups/77899021863/
Join me on Twitter: https://www.twitter.com/vanessamiller01

Books in the RAIN series

Former Rain (Book 1)

Abundant Rain (Book 2)

Latter Rain (Book 3)

Rain Storm (Book 4)

Through the Storm (Book 5)

Rain For Christmas (Book 6)

After the Rain (Book 7)

Rain in the Promised, Land (Book 8)

Sunshine and Rain (Book 9) rel. January 2016